A REVIVED

MODERN

CLASSIC

THE MAN WITH THE HEART IN THE HIGHLANDS & OTHER EARLY STORIES

ALSO BY WILLIAM SAROYAN
AVAILABLE FROM NEW DIRECTIONS

Madness in the Family
EDITED BY LEO HAMALIAN

WILLIAM SAROYAN

THE MAN WITH THE HEART IN THE HIGHLANDS & OTHER EARLY STORIES

INTRODUCTION BY HERB CAEN

A NEW DIRECTIONS BOOK

Publisher's Note: Special thanks are due to Brian Darwent, who first brought this material to New Directions' attention.
The sixteen stories in this collection originally appeared in the following volumes: *Inhale and Exhale* (1936), *Three Times Three* (1936), *Little Children* (1937), *The Trouble with Tigers* (1938), *Love, Here Is My Hat* (1938), and *Dear Baby* (1944).

Manufactured in the United States of America.

First published clothbound by New Directions in 1989, and as NDP740 in 1992
ISBN: 978-0-8112-1205-2
Library of Congress Cataloging-in-Publication Data

Saroyan, William, 1908–1981
The man with the heart in the highlands & other early stories / William Saroyan.
p. cm.—(A New Directions revived modern classic)
ISBN 0-8112-1115-0 (alk. paper)
I. Title. II. Series: Revived modern classic.
PS3537.A826M36 1989
813'.52—dc20 89-31604
CIP

FIFTH PRINTING

New Directions Books are published for James Laughlin
by New Directions Publishing Corporation,
80 Eighth Avenue, New York 10011

Contents

Introduction

BY HERB CAEN

For half a dozen unforgettable years—from, roughly, 1934 to 1940—Bill Saroyan was the king of San Francisco. He seemed to be everywhere at once—hanging out at Izzy Gomez's famous speakeasy-turned-dump on Pacific St., betting wildly on unknown racehorses at a bookie joint in Opera Alley (just off Mission on Skid Row), playing killer poker with hard-eyed gents in the back room of New Joe's restaurant on Broadway in North Beach, discussing the vagaries of life far into the night with Sally Stanford, queen of San Francisco's madams, and that was only part of his day.

When he wasn't thus engaged, he could be found riding his rusty old bike at Ocean Beach, gazing at the Pacific from his favorite perch on Red Rock in the Sunset District, and attempting to play tennis in Golden Gate Park, across the street from his small flat on Carl St. In his usual exuberant style, he would hit the ball as hard as he could, exclaiming "Look at that thing go!" When it was explained that distance was not the object, he lost interest in the game. He would then be caught browsing among the used bookstores of McAllister St., cadging drinks from tourists at the Black Cat saloon in North

Beach (also the rendezvous of such artists as Don Kingman, Beniamino Bufano, and Matt Barnes), making risque jokes with the lesbians at nearby Mona's, and being lionized by sexy socialite ladies who found his enthusiasm and dark-eyed good looks strangely fascinating.

And while doing all this, and more, he somehow found time to write. Torrents of words flowed out of his beat-up typewriter. He played that old machine like a virtuoso, with gusto and joy and not a little schmaltz. The words poured directly from his great Armenian heart onto the foolscap, effortlessly and sometimes, it seemed, without conscious thought. I saw a lot of his manuscripts during those exuberant times, and it didn't appear that he ever rewrote a line. "Rewrite what?" he would roar. "It comes out perfect." He was his own greatest fan, but not in the rather unattractive manner of Ernest Hemingway. He truly loved words—his own, in particular.

For me, a fledgling columnist for *The San Francisco Chronicle,* Bill Saroyan was a godsend—Great Copy—although he did get slightly annoyed when I called him "a shrieking violet" who suffered from "pernicious Armenia." At that time of his life, the time that peaked with his play, *The Time of Your Life,* he loved publicity and was enamored of the spotlight. He knew how to make Great Copy: when Bennet Cerf, the cofounder of Random House, checked into the Palace Hotel one day in 1936, he received a phone call from the desk clerk, who said, "A man who says he is the world's greatest writer is in the lobby." "Send Mr. Saroyan right up," said Cerf. An oft-repeated tale but I was present at the birth.

He used to read my column with a jaundiced eye. "San Francisco is a great town," he said, "but is it really worth a full column every day?" Whether it was or not, Saroyan's name was in there almost every day, to the point where readers would suggest snidely that I was in love with him—and, in a way, I was. He was not only Great Copy, he was great company. He talked as well as he wrote, in a booming voice punctuated with hearty laughter. He told rambling stories about his Armenian kinfolk that had no particular point—the same could be said of some of his writing—but were a joy to listen to anyway.

I could never decide whether he was genuinely naive or was simply putting everybody on with his bumpkin-from-Fresno act. A dashing green-eyed socialite named Anita Howard (her father-in-law owned the famous racehorse, Seabiscuit) gave a cocktail party for him in her Nob Hill penthouse, crowded with friends who wanted to meet Anita's latest catch. Two hours went by and no Saroyan. I felt sure he was going to stand her up but suddenly he breezed in to announce, "Sorry, folks, my streetcar was late." He delighted in walking into the extremely posh Lower Bar of the Mark Hopkins hotel wearing soiled tennis shoes with his customary wrinkled blue suit and carrying a greasy bag of shrimp from Fisherman's Wharf. He'd pass the bag around to one and all, roaring "Care to try some shrimp? Fresh, y'know."

Although he was indeed catnip to the ladies, the Saroyan of the late 1930s was one of the boys. He delighted in playing poker, at which he was spectacularly bad. One night at New Joe's, playing stud poker at high stakes, he bluffed everybody out except the owner of the restaurant, Joe Merello. As Merello shoved in yet another stack of chips, Saroyan advised, "Save your money, Joe, I've got aces back to back." When this proved to be true and Saroyan raked in the pot, Merello screamed, "You lied to me! You said you had aces back-to-back and you had 'em!"

Meanwhile, he kept turning out that incredible flood of words. Book after book was published, not all of them greeted as enthusiastically as his first great success, "The Daring Young

Man on the Flying Trapeze," one of the finest of all American short stories. Some critics faulted him as self-indulgent, overly sentimental and purely escapist, but his self-confidence never wavered. Expanding his oeuvre into playwriting, he wrote *The Time of Your Life*—laid in a San Francisco waterfront saloon very much like Izzy Gomez's—in six days and nights. When it won a Pulitzer Prize, he refused to accept it, a move that brought him world-wide headlines. "Who needs it anyway," he confided one day. "Now the Nobel Prize, that's different. That's real MONEY."

Bill Saroyan, the daring young man whose heart was forever in the highlands, would have been delighted to see this book. The only thing he was afraid of was being forgotten. When John Steinbeck won the Nobel Prize, he was momentarily dismayed. "Well," he said, "so the guy from Salinas beat out the guy from Fresno. I guess that means he really made it and I didn't." Then, brightening: "But I still know I'm a better writer, dammit." Saroyan was one of two writers who had a lasting effect on San Francisco. There was Dashiell Hammett, with his foggy nights of the dirty trenchcoat, mysterious shadows across the curtained windows of shabby apartments, the splash of a double-crosser's body being dropped into the dark bay. And there was Saroyan's sunny world of hookers with hearts of gold, wise old bartenders and charming Armenians with as great a gift for gab as he—people who can and did say enthusiastically, "In San Francisco, even the ugly is beautiful!"

William Saroyan's place in American letters is secure. And I think it is his San Francisco that will prevail.

THE MAN WITH THE HEART IN THE HIGHLANDS & OTHER EARLY STORIES

Secrets in Alexandria

Monday again, and the day ending: an evening paper and a ride home: 6 BILLION WORKS BILL IN SENATE. Well, yes, something was stirring. He swung aboard a B car and found a corner on the rear platform where there was room enough for him to hold the folded paper before him: U. S. TROOPS AID PEIPING GUARD IN NEW JAP DRIVE. War over there. What the hell were they fighting about, those Japs and Chinese? TANFORAN RESULTS: a horse named Royal Carlaris. SIX NOTABLES KILL SELVES IN GERMAN SUICIDE WAVE. Ernst Oberfohren, Dr. Von Bruck, Ernst and Lina Katz, Nelly Neppach, former German tennis champion. Men of quality, pistol shots, gas-filled rooms, Nazis in power. Many events, much talk, the earth turning, history emerging: he turned with hope to the theatrical page and went over the names of the neighborhood theatres, Majestic, Casino, Riviera, Parkside, El Rey, Uptown, Alhambra, Marina, Milano, Lincoln, Harding, Alexandria: his theatre: tonight: Mae West *She Done Him Wrong.*

Thoughts of Mae West, the lady of the luscious lips: madam, I admire your bust, what breasts you have.

After supper he combed his hair and put on a fresh shirt: an affair with Broadway's most glamorous female figure. In the theatre he felt renewed and at home: the day by day identity he wore fell swiftly away. He sat, waiting with quiet joy the coming of the beautiful lady. The comedy was fair and the audience laughed. It had been a hard day at the office. All day he had thought of big houses, big cars, elegant manners, money to burn, delicious ladies coming and going, and he himself standing in the midst of all this.

The lady appeared, heavy with diamonds, packed tight in her silk and velvet gown, her bosom bulging with life and whiteness, all of her being curving universally, the ocean, the everlasting waves, and that articulation, the sexual language, the passionate manner of uttering inanities: it was tremendous stuff, and he began to feel unlost, unhampered, unencumbered; and slowly but gracefully, gliding upon the line of his vision, he moved manfully to the posture of himself in Cary Grant, the hero, and he was on the screen, standing in the presence of Mae West, he the handsome young officer of the Salvation Army: the clean masculine eyes, the solidity of his flesh, the restrained fire of his being. His performance delighted him, and he kissed the buxom lady with true manly vigor, making her bend, making her pant with passion.

Then the newsreel, more events that bored him, and he emerged from the theatre. Walking home to his room he left the magnification of himself on the screen and became gradually once again David Bomerer, the bookkeeper, walking home from the Alexandria in May, feeling lousy. Where were such ladies in his world? He looked into the night faces of girls and women walking in the streets. They were pathetic. A man could not be powerful with them, a man had to be gentle, very gentle, day after day. What he wanted was that vigorous way of going about the matter, the ruthless, animal way. He felt lousy.

He passed a girl in a checkered skirt and a tight blue sweater. She had also been to the theatre, admiring Cary Grant and being Mae West. He did not turn to look into the girl's face, but walked on rapidly, as if he had a very important business engagement at ten forty-five at night. The girl lived three blocks beyond Bomerer's place, on California Street. She was a stenographer in a stock broker's office on New Montgomery Street, and she was living alone like Bomerer in a furnished room. She had a full healthy body, a fair face, and good instincts: she was longing, as she walked, with an amazing frankness, for someone strong like Cary Grant to smother her with love, not merely embraces, but the whole magnificent business, consequences and all. She watched Bomerer walking before her, and felt an intense but abstract passion for him.

A week of dictation and shorthand and typing for Ruth (Mae West) McVary: Mr. Bergerman's fat eyes upon her, and a week of virtuous devotion to Cary Grant. She rouged her lips, put on her small pert hat, and said good night to the boss. She walked with hurrying crowds to Market Street and boarded a B car. David Bomerer was standing on the rear platform reading a paper: she did not see him and went into the inside compartment of the car. Many men were seated, hiding their faces in newspapers, and she did not get a seat for fully six minutes. When the car became less crowded, beyond Fillmore Street, Bomerer entered the enclosed compartment and sat opposite Ruth McVary, holding the evening paper before him, not looking at anyone. She did not pay much attention to him: he was merely another of the many young men who happened to be alive in her time: he wasn't bad-looking at all: she read the headlines of his paper: F. R. DEMANDS, and a minute or more later when he unfolded the paper, WORLD-WIDE PEACE PLEDGE. Text of Roosevelt's Message to Rulers. President Urges All Nations to Speed Prosperity. Messages Sent to 54 Countries, Including Russia,

Asking Union for Success of Parleys. The car rambled splendidly, rolling sideways, jolting, jumping. Tonight she would take in a movie.

Tonight he would take in a movie. It was a picture he had heard a lot about and now that it had come to the neighborhood theatre he would go and see it. Helen Hayes and Gary Cooper: *Farewell to Arms.* He looked a little like Gary Cooper. Not quite as tall, but the same sort of long face, and the same sort of bewildered simplicity and sincerity. He folded a page and Ruth McVary saw a photograph of Miriam Hopkins, smiling. How beautiful she was! Bomerer put away the evening paper and began to stare at the car-card advertisements, not reading them, merely looking, and there was something so desperate about the way he did so that he reminded Ruth McVary of someone in the movies. It made her smile with tenderness for him, merely to watch him being bored and lonely. He looked to be a fine fellow, the sort of boy she could go for in a big way, giving him everything and not asking for anything. She felt a fierce impulse to be alone with him in a room with a bed, to have him love her with that desperation on his face, the solemn anger and bewilderment. She must be very lonely to have such thoughts, she thought. He got up and left the car and from where she sat she saw him walk down the street, still seeming to be desperate and angry, full of strength that needed to be released. For an instant she wanted to get up and run after him, saying to him, Listen, I understand all about it. Come along with me. We'll rent a small apartment and you can stay as long as you like. You won't have to bother about marrying me. We'll just stay together until you don't want to any more.

She got off the car and walked slowly to her room, thinking of him, wondering why, somehow, it never came about so simply, the way it ought to come about, why such decent things had been made to seem vile and why so much fake importance had been attached to them: engagements, fake love talk, marriage licenses, church ceremonies, ritual, nonsense. Why had they made such a thing so ugly and unnatural? After all, people did the same thing whether they were married or not and most married people were really pretty ugly about it. She remembered her sister, giving her advice: *Keep your husband, when you marry one, in his place. Don't give yourself as if you came at a dime a dozen.* All that deceit and filthiness, and then doing it when they really didn't care for one another. What sort of decency did they call that, anyway?

They were in the theatre together, separated by four rows of seats, seeing the same old war, this time from the Italian front, the same old passion, male for female, female for male, the boom of big guns, the horror of mass death, and amid it all these two people, big Gary Cooper, the American lieutenant in the Italian Army, and little Helen Hayes, the nurse, meeting one another accidentally, needing one another desperately, the soldier being shy like most decent Americans and the nurse being decent but honest like most clean-hearted women, and the two of them loving one another, and amid all the pain and death the little nurse conceiving, a child to be born where death was the major business, and then that black lake, as frightening as the lake of dreams, and the soldier rowing across the lake, desperate with worry, and then those scenes in the hospital, and the death of Helen Hayes, and the horror of Gary Cooper, and heavy rain coming down: Bomerer almost cried and tears came to the eyes of Ruth McVary: it was beautiful. They went sadly to their rooms, and in the morning they got up and returned to their work.

There was something about being alive . . . it was splendid . . . the persistence of fundamental feelings in spite of manufactured conditions, wars, mass hatred by propaganda:

all the young men who died without knowing love, all that waste, and the pompous bigwigs who afterwards wrote their memoirs and tried to speak like good Christians, the sons of bitches.

Farewell to Arms made them feel splendid for weeks. They began to understand how miraculous it was merely to be alive. They went back and forth from their rooms to the places where they worked, and each of them clung desperately to the ideal of that free and innocent love, decent and artless, that had existed between the lanky soldier and the tiny nurse . . . it was splendid. Even if it had been sad, there was something about that affair that was holy.

One evening, standing on the rear platform of a B car, Bomerer saw a photograph of J. P. Morgan with Lya Graf, a midget woman, sitting on his knees. The picture was labeled Sitting in the Lap of Luxury, and the news item said Titan Poses with Midget. J. P. Morgan Snapped With Tiny Woman, Blushes Furiously. More events. Heywood Broun had something to say about the House of Morgan. Long articles about inflation. What did all that stuff have to do with him? He turned impatiently to the theatrical page. At the Alexandria: *Sign of the Cross* Elissa Landi and Fredric March: boy, that ought to be great.

In the theatre, in the seat to his left, sat a woman whose face he could not make out clearly in the dark. The picture was about Christians in Rome and what they suffered. He had never imagined that such things had actually taken place, Christians being fed to lions. It was very exciting and now and then the things that happened made him so angry he wanted to say something out loud, especially when they began to torture the little Christian boy. And it was the same with the woman who sat beside him. Once, unable to contain herself, the woman clutched his knee nervously, uttering some emotional exclamation, and he held her hand tightly, feeling with her the pain suffered by the Christians, and feeling at the same time a little awkward and ugly. He did not again release her hand, and belong long they were pressing their calves together, tingling with the touch of one another.

They emerged from the theatre together, and he saw that the woman was not young, not at all good-looking, a woman in her late thirties, heavy, sex-faced, and yet he knew he wanted her and that he wouldn't let her get away from him. The woman had a similar idea of her own, and she led him deftly in the direction of her house, a flat on Twenty-seventh Street. They talked about the Christians of those times, what terrible things they suffered, and their resentment grew until it became something vast. They felt angry and powerful about the Christians suffering, and Bomerer wanted very much to embrace this woman and make her feel how much he hated those people who had done the cruel things to the Christians.

He didn't like the smell of the woman's flat. She extended her fat breasts toward him the instant they got inside and he put his arms around her awkwardly, pressing his lips to hers. Some of her spittle got on his lips and he felt unclean. She asked him to make himself at home in the parlor while she got him a drink, and she closed a door behind her, smiling at him fatly. He got out a cigarette in a hurry and began to inhale, feeling bewildered and ashamed. He hadn't wanted *this* and he was being dishonest. She probably meant to get into looser clothes. He began to walk about in the room, feeling more lost than ever before, and unconsciously he began to walk to the door and back again to the window.

When the woman returned, he was not in the room. She had sprayed some perfume on her face and bosom, and put on a pair of pink beach pajamas. She sat down sullenly and thought, God damn fool.

Walking home, he hoped he would never see the woman again.

Day after day Ruth McVary looked for him among the people on B car, and one Saturday evening in June he entered again the enclosed compartment of the car and sat down. He was still bored and he still held the evening paper before him, and she knew that somehow, even if she had to make a fool of herself, she would get to know him. She hadn't thought of another person for more than a month. There was something about his bewilderment that made her want him desperately. She would have to make him understand that she was what he needed. The part of the paper toward her said Balbo, Mussolini's Right-Hand Man, Leads Italian Air Armada to Chicago. Brewer Taken by Kidnapers. World Needs U. S. Aid, Says Trotzky.

When he left the car she followed him. She stood across the street from the rooming house in which he lived until he emerged after an hour. She felt her hunger rise, her stomach groaning, and then pass, being overwhelmed by a far greater hunger than hunger for food. He walked slowly in the direction of the neighborhood theatre. She hoped he would go in because in the darkness, with the moving picture going on, she would find it easier to have her life touch his, to make a beginning. He went straight to the box-office, purchased a ticket, and entered the theatre. She followed him swiftly, and although hardly anyone was in the theatre she sat in the same row, one seat away from him. The picture was *Peg O' My Heart* with Marion Davies, a beautiful Irish story with lovely songs. After a while the theatre began to fill with people and when two people sought seats in her row she was forced to move over and take the seat beside him. Her heart began to beat noisily, and as the picture unfolded she tried to make him understand what a splendid spirit she had and how much she wanted him to know that spirit.

She laughed beautifully at Marion Davies's witty Irish remarks, and when the star sang *Sweetheart, Darlin'* her shoulder somehow just barely touched his, and she made no effort to change her position. She waited breathlessly for a return of the pressure, but instead she felt his shoulder moving away, and the delicate tension of the touch was broken.

Bomerer thought, No more of that sort of thing for me.

The feature ended. Still, she had not yet got anywhere near him, and now here was this absurd comedy that was without tenderness, without sincerity, altogether vulgar and stupid. If he could only understand how it was with her, how much she loved him, how important his sadness and bewilderment were to her. Well, she would *make* him understand. Why should two young people have a lot of silly pride? Why shouldn't she humble herself and go to him whether he liked it or not? Now the newsreel was being shown and she could tell from his restlessness that in a moment he would get up and go away. And that would be the end of it. The rotten end. There was nothing fine in the newsreel, nothing that could bring his mind into some fine relationship to hers, so how was she to touch him? Then suddenly she saw that a Baby Parade was being shown. Babies. Beautiful children. She forced her hand to fall, as if accidentally, on his knee, trembling. He did not take her hand into his own and after an imperceptible duration of time she drew it away nervously, blushing with shame and anger. He got up quickly and went away, all her hope and desire crumbling and smashing to the turning of the Paramount Camera on the screen.

She could not move. She felt cold and ugly and broken-hearted, really broken-hearted. The feature began again and she began to see again what she had already seen, Peg and her father in Ireland, her Ireland, living their simple lives, being happy, talking and singing, and she felt a great longing for that life, and then suddenly that sad Irish boy with the small accordion began to sing *We'll Remember,* and everything was so mean and ugly, and yet there were these beautiful things somewhere and they were always out of her life and everything she had ever wanted that was decent and beautiful had never come to be and it was always like this, everybody lonely, no one being able to touch another's life, and she began to cry softly to herself in the darkness of the theatre, still yearning desperately for the young man who would have made her life beautiful, still wanting to become a part of his desperation and bewilderment.

The Younger Brother

I thank you for having been my sister and I am sorry it has turned out this way where I am writing a letter to you like this not like a brother only you know as well as I do why I am doing this. I do not like to write like this because it makes me remember the times when things were different and then I get mad and can't sit still and I start to drink too much the way you said I was always a drunkard and you know that's a lie. I only drink when I don't know what to do and that's because I feel so bad.

You know I never was a fellow to cry and when I feel bad the way I feel when everything looks bad I can't sit down like other people and cry and then feel all right because I know everything will never be all right and what's the use to cry? I drink a little because it burns me up to see everything going wrong in our lives and after I have a couple of drinks I feel better for a little while and I don't care what happens.

I got back to Frisco this afternoon at four and it is now a little after midnight and I have had a couple of drinks again. I don't like to drink and be like this but I don't know what to do and I remember everything when we lived in the house on San Carlo Street in Kingsburg and Papa and Mama were there, and I keep remembering how you were my favorite sister the only person who would stick up for me and tell everybody leave him alone, leave Jimmy alone. I was hungry when I got back to Frisco and I walked around town trying to get over feeling bad but it was no use and I felt homesick, so I couldn't eat. The weather was fine all afternoon and if I didn't feel so bad I guess I would have had a good meal and tried to start over again, but I kept remembering how fine it was in the old house and I didn't know what to do. I had one or two drinks in the afternoon and then I started to drink more and more to forget only now I am sober again because I walked along Embarcadero and the clean air made me wake up. I hurried uptown to the Y.M.C.A. where I am writing this letter to thank you for being my sister when we were in the house with Papa and Mama because I remember how good you were in those days. I feel bad and I don't like to write like this but I am sober again and I have enough money for room rent tonight and meals tomorrow and after that I don't care what happens I guess. Lots of funny things have been happening and I don't care what happens to me because I feel bad about everything.

I want you to know that I am not your brother any more and you are not my sister because you are changed and Papa and Mama are dead and another family lives in the house on San Carlo Street and all of you are married and settled down except me. I didn't care when Steve got married because Steve was always making fun of me because I never did know what to do and didn't like to work like a slave in a packing house and I didn't care when Rosa got married because Rosa was always saying I was lazy and good for nothing just because I wanted to do something only I didn't know what, but when you got married to Nick Renna I got a little afraid because that left me alone in the house. I had a job at Guggenheim's and I could pay the twelve dollars a month rent but I was all alone. You said you would come over and help me out but after the first month you stopped coming over and all I had to eat was canned beans and hot dogs and things like that and when I asked you to come over again and cook me a meal like Mama used to cook you said you couldn't because you were going to have a baby and Nick got tough and said he didn't want me to bother you and this made me so mad I couldn't help it and I lost my temper because Papa and Mama were dead and everything was changing and I had that first fight with Nick. I didn't mean to hurt him but I guess I lost control of myself because he didn't understand that you were my best sister and that next to Papa and Mama you were the one who was always trying to let me figure things out for myself.

I walked around town all afternoon feeling homesick and knowing we didn't have the house any more and wondering why everything was going wrong, and then I started to drink. I can't believe everything is really this way and I keep remembering the house as if all of us were still there, Papa at the table pouring wine and Mama filling our plates with real Italian food and all of us laughing and having a good home to live in. I was fifteen when Papa died and you were sixteen and all week you cried and I didn't go to school because it was too terrible and I stayed home and tried to keep you from crying because even after we came home from the funeral I couldn't believe Papa was really dead and I thought as long as we could be in his house he could not be dead and I didn't cry not even at the funeral when everybody else was crying. I felt sick inside and I knew it was hurting Mama but I couldn't cry because Papa was a man who was always laughing and I didn't believe he was dead.

After the third fight with Nick when they put me in jail for two weeks I felt so bad about everything and so ashamed of myself for sending him to the hospital just when you were going to have your first baby that I had to quit my job at Guggenheim's and leave our house and move to Frisco where I always thought I would like to live. You and Steve and Rosa got all the furniture and I moved to Frisco and got a job in a warehouse moving things around because it was the only job I could get and I had no money. I was almost nineteen and I said to myself it was time for me to forget everything and believe exactly what had happened to all of us and I tried to do it. I worked hard and pleased my bosses but I never did like the work and you know I was always wanting to do something different not just the same things everybody else was doing and maybe if I hadn't I would be much better off now only I couldn't help it. I thought some day I would find out what I wanted to do and I would get along all right but I guess it's all over now.

And less than a year after Papa died Mama died and that was a terrible time because Papa and Mama were born in Italy and we were born in Kingsburg and then we had nothing. I mean Papa and Mama were always telling us about the old country and we knew they had lived there. I mean it was good to know that Papa and Mama had lived in Italy. I'm not drunk any more but I mean when Mama died it was a terrible time because none of us had lived in Italy and we didn't know about it the way Papa and Mama did and I knew it would never be the same with us again. I could feel it a week after Mama's funeral when Steve began to pick on me and Papa wasn't there to tell him to shut up and Mama wasn't there to tell him to let me alone and you didn't say anything because you said Steve was the oldest and he was boss. Steve was the oldest but he wasn't like Papa and I couldn't help it if I said some mean things to him and had all those fights. I always liked Steve but he was not like Papa and I was glad when he got married and moved away.

They always told us at school to work hard and please the bosses and we would be able to work up to a better job and I tried to do it, but I never did like working in a warehouse because it didn't seem to be the kind of work I needed to do and one day I got into an argument with Mr. Fielding the foreman and he called me a Wop and I had a bad fight with him. He was a big man and everybody in the warehouse was afraid of him but when he called me a Wop and looked at me the way he did I couldn't think of anything else to do and I had to fight him. It was a big fight and he gave me a bad beating but I made his nose bleed and I knocked him down twice and everybody said it served him right because he was a coward anyway. He was always making cracks at the fellows and everybody was afraid to call his bluff but he got me sore and I was sick and tired of the job anyway so I had to do something. I knew I didn't want to work in a warehouse all my life and I didn't want to quit because that would seem foolish so when he called me a Wop I had this fight with Mr. Fielding and they fired me.

I have been writing for two hours now and the clerk has just come over to my table and asked if I wanted to rent a room for the night or what, and I told him no, I just wanted to write a letter and he went away, so I guess I had better hurry and finish this letter. I told him I would pay for the letter paper and the envelope but he said it was free, but I guess they don't like it when a fellow takes so long to write a letter. It is almost two thirty now and I guess I won't go to bed tonight because I wouldn't be able to sleep anyway because I keep remembering all of us in the house on San Carlo Street and I can't believe everything is like this now, Papa and Mama dead and all of you married and me always in trouble.

When I quit the job at the warehouse I had eighty dollars in the bank and I was beginning to feel homesick, so I went back to Kingsburg and I will tell you what I was thinking of doing. I was thinking of renting our house again and finding a job for myself and getting married. I had been away almost two years and when I got back everything was so changed I couldn't believe it. I went back to our old house before I visited you and Nick and it didn't seem the same at all. I couldn't tell what had happened to it but it didn't seem the same and I didn't know what to do. I said to myself that maybe if I moved in again and got back some of the old furniture it would be the same again, so I went to the front door and rang the bell and the people who live there opened the door and asked me what I wanted. I told them it was our house first. I mean we didn't own it but we had rented it for twenty years, and I asked them in Italian if they were going to stay in the house very much longer. There was a man and his wife and four or five kids and the man said it was a good house and he was going to stay in it a long time. I didn't know what to think because I saw our parlor from the door, all changed, different furniture and different pictures on the wall, and I thought it was wrong. I said to myself I had no right to move away from the house and go to Frisco because Papa and Mama had lived there so long and I asked the man if he would let me walk through the house. He laughed and his wife laughed but they invited me in and I went through every room, all the places where we had lived and then I don't know what happened and I got sick to my stomach because everything was so changed and for the first time in my life I wanted to cry and I almost did. I had to try like anything to keep the tears from coming out of my eyes, and the people were smiling and laughing about me until they noticed how bad I was feeling and then they stopped smiling and the man began to act nervous and he poured me a glass of wine.

I told him I had been in Frisco almost two years and this was the house we had lived in so long. Then I went away. Walking from our old house to your house I felt very bad and I wanted to know if we could ever get the things back that we have lost and I said to myself maybe Elena will understand why I have come back and it won't be so bad any more because she will remember with me how it used to be, but you know what happened and all the trouble I got into and the way you shouted at me and called me names and stuck up for Nick who always hated me, and you were so changed I couldn't believe it and I knew it was all over. I rented that small house in our old neighborhood for a month because I wanted to be near where we had lived, but it was no use I couldn't get a job anywhere and almost all of my money was gone, so I came back to Frisco.

I want to explain why I came to your house the night before I left Kingsburg because maybe you and Nick thought I came to borrow money or stay with you. I had eleven dollars that night and there was no place for me to go, but I didn't come to your house for money or a place to sleep. I only wanted to see if I could talk to you the way it used to be because if I knew you hadn't changed then I wouldn't have to feel so bad about everything, and even if I went away I would always know that you remembered and it would make up for a lot of the other things. You know that when Papa was worrying about something he sometimes got drunk and Mama never did call him names and I guess I was a little drunk too. I only wanted to know that you were not changed but I was so afraid you were changed that I had to drink a little and maybe I drank too much. You know the rest. How you and Nick picked on me from the beginning and got me so sore I had to have another fight with Nick. I wasn't sore at Nick. I was sore because you were changed and everything was finished. So I am writing to apologize to Nick. It wasn't his fault.

It is now half past three and this letter is much longer than I thought it would be, but I thought I ought to tell you I remember how you were once my sister and I am sorry it has turned out like this with everything broken to pieces. I have a little money left and I guess I'll be able to get along all right but I don't care much what happens one way or another.

I want to thank you for sticking up for me when we lived in the house on San Carlo Street and I don't want you to think I am sore or anything because I am not. I came back to Kingsbury to see if we couldn't save something, but I guess we can't, so I might as well forget everything and the only way I can do it is by telling you I am not your brother any more and you are not my sister any more.

The Mother

One morning in June he saw the girl who lived in one of the furnished rooms across the street coming down the steps of the house, and moving toward her as she came slowly down the steps he noticed a strange quiet joy in her expression and decided something fine had happened to her. She came slowly down the steps because it was her way, being one of the slow-moving and long-living races, northern and blond, and unconsciously he began walking slower, slow enough to meet her when she reached the sidewalk, and have a walk with her to the corner where they would get a street car and ride to the city.

He said good morning and walked to the corner, asking if she didn't think it was a swell morning, a warm sun, clear air, and all that, and she laughed and said it sure was. He helped her aboard the street car, touching her elbow, wondering what had happened to her, making so much of a difference, and decided it must be no more than the weather, but early in September he saw that she was pregnant, and thought to himself *holy cow,* because he knew she was living alone.

He waited a week, wondering how she would get out of it

and whether there was something he might do, and at last he went up to her room one evening with a new novel, to talk to her, tell her not to worry, anything, just so he wouldn't sit back and wait for her grief and misery and pain or anything else it might be. He knocked at her door and when she opened it he saw that her growth had increased enough to be a worry and she was more bewildered alone in her room than he would have imagined from seeing her in the street, and she was amazed to see him, of all people.

I thought you might like this book, he said, and going into her room he began wanting a cigarette badly because it was one of those rooms that made you feel lousy, and with the first lungful of smoke he himself began to feel the complete strangeness of the whole routine of living, instinctive longings impelling the weary and lost into variations of life full of pain and fear. He watched her smile, saying ordinary things with much implication, and making him want to be with her as some accompaniment to the pain until she would be free again, delivered of the primary and endless complication of living, a new life. He understood from the quiet fullness of her glance, thick with brooding and loneliness and at the same time inevitable joy and amazement, and from her acceptance of his gift and his presence in the room, that she understood why he had come, so he decided not to ask any question, though he believed the whole thing was fine enough, even if the man was nowhere around, or maybe married, and all he could do was inhale and exhale smoke and smile at her, his smiling meaning somehow, because of the growth in her and her sad presence in the small room and himself there, a witness to the incipient third, all the decent things a man could never say in words, Oh, do not be afraid, do not be ashamed, the Queen of England pregnant is no more than you, and maybe something less, so do not be afraid.

Being in the room with her in the dim light, in the smallness of the place, the secrecy of it, he felt quietly happy, not joyous, not pleased, but deeply glad, and hearing her voice, innocently, he could feel the truth of his life becoming the truth of her life, and somehow he began to feel related to the child growing within her, but going away from her this feeling changed and he became angry about the girl's predicament. He decided he would not see her again, since no good could come from such an arrangement, and the following evening he sat alone in his room, across the street from the house in which she sat alone and listened to phonograph records.

It happens a thousand times a day all over the earth, he said, and it will go on happening forever. A thousand of them will groan tonight with the mad pain of giving life, and they will be alone. What am I to her? Do the muscles of the king ache with the queen's suffering? What is she to the man who is gone, or to the child who is coming? It is all loneliness.

And the music of the phonograph records, which his ear knew as thoroughly as his eye knew the shape and meaning of his room, became bitterly sad, like wailing. He wondered if she might be weeping, and without thinking, without even shutting off the phonograph, without coat or hat, he rushed from the room, went down the steps two and three at a time, ran across the street, thinking she must not weep, up the stairs, swiftly up the hall, knowing he was being a fool, and knocked quietly at her door.

She was amazed to see him, no hat, no coat, his face sullen, angry, his mouth bitter with speechlessness, and when he was in the room all he could think was that he had forgotten his cigarettes, which he needed badly, since without them he knew he would talk, and talk like a fool, and he said, How are you, anyway? I've been thinking about you. You aren't afraid, are you? Don't be afraid. If you don't mind, I'll come over every night. You aren't alone. Do you want to walk in the park Sunday if it is a good day? Have you enough money for the hospital? I have all kinds of money. Are you seeing a doctor? Don't get any silly ideas in your head because I live across the street and if you feel like it you can tell everybody I'm the guy. I don't want you to be afraid or ashamed because it's an old thing and it happens a thousand times a night. Do you like movie magazines? All you girls seem to like love stories. Do you want me to bring you a half dozen magazines with love stories in them?

Jesus Christ, he said, I need a drink. Don't mind what I'm saying. Would you like to have my phonograph and records? You could listen to music and it would help you wait.

He watched her while he spoke, then became angry with himself, doing a crazy thing, being a fool, seeing her want to cry, and he began to swear sullenly. God damn it the hell, how are you, anyway? he said.

The landlady says I've got to go, she said, and began to cry silently.

He jumped up like a crazy man, hating the landlady and all her tribe, all the pettiness in people, the imposed pitilessness in people, their fear, their love of conventions, husband, wife, and child, legally, and he said, almost roaring, Do you think I give a God damn about the landlady or anybody else? Do you think I care what they think? You don't need to cry. You don't need to be afraid, I won't let them make you ashamed. You're not alone. I live across the street, don't I? I like you, don't I? I'll get you out of this dump. I got all kinds of money. I'll get you into a swell apartment. You can tell everybody I'm the guy. You can say we're married, and after it's all over we'll get married if you feel like it. I'll find a swell apartment the first thing in the morning. I'll bring you a dozen magazines with love stories in them. I'll trade in my old phonograph for an orthophonic and I'll bring you a lot of swell records. You wouldn't care for operas, would you? I'll bring popular stuff, anything you like. I'll get you a radio. You don't have to cry. You aren't alone. I live across the street and in the morning I'll find an apartment for you. If you want me to stay in the apartment, I'll stay. If you don't, I won't. I like you, but if you don't like me, you're not alone just the same. I'll bring you the swellest bunch of love stories you ever read. Don't sit there and cry as if you were all alone in the world.

And he began walking up and down the room like a panther in a cage, and the poor girl cried and cried.

At last she stopped crying and began to talk. I'd go home, she said, but my father would kill me. I've saved up a hundred dollars and I'm going to see a doctor. I can get another job just as soon as I get well again. I don't want a baby.

And then she began to cry again.

No, he said. You don't want a baby. Oh, no, not much. You want a baby more than anything else in the world. Not much you don't want a baby. I'm telling you everything will be all right. You can say I'm the guy. I'm telling you you can.

And the more he talked the more she cried, and he could feel how much she wanted to see the life growing in her, a baby, outside, her own life, and he kept telling her he would get her into a swell apartment and buy a fine phonograph for her and dozens of magazines with love stories in them, and from the way she cried he could tell he was wasting time because she wasn't going to let him do it, the crazy way little stenographers could be, just like all people, willing to accept conventions and be frightened by talk.

God damn your landlady, he said. Who in hell does she think she is, God or somebody?

When he got back to his room he knew he didn't love the

girl. Sure, he didn't, but that wasn't the point. It wasn't a question of love, it was a question of letting her have her baby, and Jesus Christ he was a fool, oh, he was the God damnedest fool that ever lived. Why didn't he forget the whole business and let her do anything she pleased? Why should he be making so much of a fuss over a little girl who happened to be knocked up? Jesus Christ. It happened a thousand times a day and nobody gave a good God damn. Nobody minded if the girls got themselves mangled getting rid of their unborn babies. No, he had to be a swell guy. He had to want to do the right thing just because he lived across the street from her and had seen how happy the beginning of the growth had made her. He had to be a pal to her, telling her he had all kinds of money when all he had was enough to barely get by on. He had to pretend he loved her and everything else. A dozen magazines full of love stories, a radio, an orthophonic phonograph, so she could feel that she wasn't alone and not be afraid or ashamed. He had to be a good guy.

Nevertheless, he rented a small apartment in the morning, and felt glad about it. Just the place for her, he said. A good view from the windows, and enough room to move around in, waiting. In the evening he went up to her room and knocked, but there was no answer, not even after he had knocked five times, each time a little harder than the time before, so that the fifth time he was making a loud noise and feeling mad as hell, knowing something dirty had happened, God damn the lousy people who embarrassed pregnant girls.

The landlady came up the hall in a hurry, very angry about the noise he was making, and when he saw her he thought he would tell her plenty, but somehow he couldn't do it because the landlady had an air about her that wouldn't let him do it: *the landlady was right, he was wrong*. Sure, that's what it came to. The world was right, he was wrong. It was proper to be unkind to pregnant girls. There were conventions. There were ways of doing things, having babies. He was a fool.

What's happened to this girl? he asked the landlady, pointing at the locked door of the girl's room.

She's gone, said the landlady. Are you the man who lives across the street? She asked me to give you a letter.

And the landlady made a face at him. You're probably the one who got her into trouble, the landlady's face said: now get her out of it. She made her bed, let her lie in it. What a man sows, he reaps. All the tripe you could think of in the meanness of her expression. No cheap girl is going to ruin the reputation of my rooming house.

Where has she gone? he asked.

I haven't the slightest idea, said the landlady. She asked me to give you this letter, if you're the man who lives across the street.

I am, he said.

She handed him the letter. She was very angry about the whole business. Are you the man who . . . ?

Maybe I am and maybe I'm not, he said. What's that got to do with it? Do you think it happens differently because they aren't married?

He opened the envelope before the landlady and read a swiftly scrawled note: she was going away, and would never see him again. The note was not signed, and he suddenly remembered he had never bothered to ask the girl her last name. He knew her first name was Esther.

What is this girl's last name? he asked the landlady, and the landlady said she didn't know for sure, the girl had given the name Vargas, but the landlady didn't believe Vargas was her real name.

He went across the street to his room and wondered what he ought to do. He had paid a month's rent on the apartment, all furnished and ready to live in, and now this crazy girl had run off and would probably get herself into a terrible mess trying to get the growth out of herself before it was ready to come out naturally.

He bought a copy of the Sunday *Examiner* late Saturday afternoon, and turning to the *Personals* column, he read his message to her:

Esther, don't be a fool. Apartment rented. I love you. Joe.

There was no answer to his message, not even in the *Personals* column. September ended, October ended, Christmas came, the year ended, and all during the excitement of the ending year he could think of nothing but the girl, wondering where she could be, and if she killed the growth, or had the baby, and January ended, and February, and one day in March, while he was out on Market Street during his lunch hour, he bumped into her, his heart leaping a mile high because he had been thinking about her so much, and she was very neat, working again, and when he saw her he saw how it had ended and he felt sore as they make them because he could tell from the way she looked, even after it was all over, that she had wanted that baby more than anything else in the world, and was herself partly dead because the baby was, too.

All the same, she was glad to see him, and standing together in the middle of the sidewalk, with people swarming all around them, they talked a moment, knowing how it was, and making this accidental meeting a casual and a most unimportant event. A minute of ordinary talk, and yet when the sudden renewed relationship between them, as if they might still be in her small room, with the growth still accumulating in her, was about to end, each of them going on alone, the girl said, I read your message in the *Examiner*. (People hurrying by: they would not be standing together long.) It was so funny, she said. (In another moment they would no longer be together.) It was so nice of you to say you loved me. (I will bring you a dozen magazines full of love stories.) Well, she said, goodbye. (And then she could feel herself turning her back to him, losing sight of his furious and bewildered stare, going away from him as if it simply had to be that way, and it was the very same with him, though he knew definitely that he had never loved the girl, and he could feel himself walking swiftly away from her, thinking, Baby, I love you, oh, that is funny, ha ha. And the place where they had stood together in the city was for a moment one of the most desolate places of the earth, and then several people jostled the ghosts that had been standing there sullenly, and the sadness of the place was swept away by the movement of thousands of the living, hurrying up the street and down.)

The Living and the Dead

I

I was in my room fast asleep at three in the afternoon when Pete the writer came in without knocking. I knew it was Pete from the extra nervous way the door opened and I didn't need to open my eyes to make sure who it was *after* he was in because I could smell it was somebody who needed a bath and I couldn't remember anyone I knew who needed one, except Pete, so I tried to stay asleep. I knew he wanted to talk and if there was anything I didn't want to be bothered with at that hour of the day it was talk.

When you are asleep at an hour when everybody but a loafer is supposed to be awake you understand how foolish all the activity and talk of the world is and you have an idea the world would be a better place in which to suffer if everybody would stop talking a while and go to sleep. You figure sleep is one of the extra special privileges of the mortal. You figure not being able to sleep is the basic cause of man's jumping around in the world, trying to do stuff.

It was a warm day and the light of the sun was on my face,

going through my shut eyes to the measureless depths of the rest of it, the past of my life, the place where the past is assembled, lighting up this vast area inside, and I was feeling quiet as a rock and very truthful. Try it sometime. Maybe you have no idea how far away you've been from where you are now, within your skull and skin, but if you are alive and know it, chances are you've been everywhere and seen everything and have just reached home, and my slogan is this: What this world needs is a better understanding of how and when to sleep. Anybody can be awake, but it takes a lot of quiet oriental wisdom to be able to lay your weary body in the light of the sun and remember the beginning of the earth.

Pete isn't a bad guy and in his own way he can write a simple sentence that sometimes means what he wants it to mean. Ordinarily, in spite of the smell, he is good company. He is excited, but that's because he is trying hard to say something that will straighten out everything and make everybody get up tomorrow morning with a clean heart and a face all furrowed with smiles.

Asleep, I am a profound thinker. Awake, however, I am a picture of good breeding.

There were two quart bottles of cheap beer on the table, a bottle-opener, a glass, and a package of Chesterfields. Pete opened a bottle, poured himself a glass, took a gulp, lit a cigarette, inhaled, and I sat up and yawned, my only form of exercise.

God Almighty, Pete said, how can you sleep at a time like this. Don't you realize the world is going mad? How can you stretch out in this hole in the wall and sleep? Do you mind if I have a drink?

I told him anything I had was his, and he said: The true bourgeois, all kindness, but you can't fool me. That sort of charity isn't going to stand in the way of the revolution. They are trying to buy us off with their cheap groceries and their free rent, but we'll rise up and crush them.

I yawned and opened the window. A little clean air moved past the curtain and I breathed it and yawned again. Who do you want to crush? I said.

Don't be funny, said Pete. This tyranny's got to end. They're trying to cram Fascism down our throats, but they won't get away with it.

Who are you talking about? I said.

The bosses, said Pete, the lousy bosses.

You haven't done an honest day's work in ten years, I said. What bosses?

The rats, said Pete. The blood-sucking Capitalists. Morgan and Mellon and them big pricks.

Them guys are just as pathetic as you are, I said. I'll bet ten to one if you could meet Morgan you'd appreciate how close to death he is. He'd give two or three million dollars to be in your boots, just so he wouldn't have to be a writer. He'd give every penny he has to be as young as you are. Morgan's an old man. He isn't long for this world. He'll be dead any minute now. You've got a good forty years ahead of you if you don't fall down somewhere and bust your head against a fire hydrant.

That's all bourgeois talk, said Pete. I'm talking about *twenty-five million hungry men, women and children in America.*

He poured himself another glass of beer and spilled some of the foam on to his vest and wiped it off and said he wished to Christ I wouldn't be a Fascist and be an honest Communist and work toward international goodwill among men.

I'm no Fascist, I said. I don't even know what the word means.

Means? said Pete. You don't know what Fascism means?

I'll tell you what it means. It means muzzling the press. It means the end of free speech. The end of free thinking.

Well, that isn't so bad, I said. A man can always get by without free speech. There isn't much to say anyway. Living won't stop when free speech does. Everybody except a few public debaters will go right on living the same as ever. Wait and see. We won't miss the debaters.

That's a lot of hooey, said Pete. Do you mind if I have another cigarette?

You're excited, I said. What's on your mind?

Confidentially, said Pete, I've been sent out by the local chapter of the Party to get a dollar from you.

Oh, I said. I thought you were really upset about the poor.

I *am*, said Pete.

What do they want a dollar for? I said.

To help get out the next number of the *Young Worker*, said Pete.

Young Worker, my eye, I said. *Young Loafer*. You babies never worked in your lives, and what's more you don't even know how to loaf.

I got a story in the next number, said Pete.

That cinches it, I said. I hope they never raise the money to get the paper out.

It's the best story I ever wrote, said Pete.

And that's none too good, I said.

It's the sort of story that will tear out their rotten hearts, said Pete.

Have another beer, I said. Open the other bottle. That's what you think. You've got twenty or thirty dopes down there who want to be writers. Communism is a school of writing to you guys.

I say plenty in this story, said Pete. I talk right out in this one.

What do you say? I said.

I say plenty, said Pete. Wait till you read it. It's called *No More Hunger Marches.*

I'll wait, I said, gladly.

You've got to let me have a dollar, said Pete. I haven't collected a dollar in six weeks and they're checking up on me.

Suppose you never collect a dollar? I said.

I'm supposed to be an active member, said Pete.

A militant member, I said.

Yeah, said Pete.

You boys are fighting *some* war, I said. Here's a dollar. Get the hell out of here. Bring me a copy of your story when it's printed. You may be Dostoyevsky in disguise. You smell bad enough to be somebody great. When are you going to take another bath?

Day after tomorrow, said Pete. Thanks for the dollar. Do you think I like going around this way, dirty clothes, no money, no baths? Under Communism we'll have bathtubs all over the place.

Under Communism, I said, you'll be exactly the way you are now, only you'll be just a little worse as a writer because there won't be anything to tear out their rotten hearts with and there won't be any rotten hearts to tear out. I was sleeping when you busted into this place. Why don't you guys send out circular letters instead of making personal calls?

Can't pay the postage, said Pete. Do you mind if I take three or four cigarettes?

Take the package, I said.

He went to the door and then turned round a little more excited than ever.

They want you to come to the meeting tonight, he said. They asked me to extend a special invitation to you to attend tonight's meeting.

You guys make me laugh, I said.

This isn't one of those boring meetings, said Pete. This is going to be better than a movie. We've got a very witty talker tonight.

I'm going to be playing poker tonight, I said. I can learn more about contemporary economics playing poker.

I'll be expecting you at the meeting, said Pete.

I may drop around, I said. If I lose at poker, I'll *be sure* to drop around. If I win, I'll want to stay in the game and see if I can't win enough to get out of town.

Everybody wants you to join the Party, said Pete. Communism needs guys with a sense of humor.

They want dues, I said.

Well, you could do at least that much for your fellow man, couldn't you?

I always tip the barber and the bootblack and the waitress, I said. Once a week I give a newsboy a half-dollar for a paper. I'm doing my little bit.

That's bourgeois talk, said Pete. I'll see you at the meeting.

If I lose at poker, I said.

He closed the door behind him and hurried down the hall. I opened all three windows of the room and breathed deeply. The sun was still shining and I stretched out again and began to sleep again.

II

Then my grandmother came into the room and stared bitterly at everything, grumbling to herself and lifting a book off the table, opening it, studying the strange print and closing it with an angry and impatient bang, as if nothing in the world could be more ridiculous than a book.

I knew she wanted to talk, so I pretended to be asleep.

My grandmother is a greater lady than any lady I have ever had the honor of meeting, and she may even be the greatest lady alive in the past-seventy class for all I know, but I always say there is a time and place for everything. They are always having baby contests in this crazy country, but I never heard of a grandmother contest. My old grandmother would walk away with every silver loving cup and gold or blue ribbon in the world in a grandmother contest, and I like her very much, but I wanted to sleep. She can't read or write, but what of it? She knows more about life than John Dewey and George Santayana put together, and that's plenty. You could ask her what's two times two and she'd fly off the handle and tell you not to irritate her with childish questions, but she's a genius just the same.

Forty years ago, she said, they asked this silly woman Oskan to tell about her visit to the village of Gultik and she got up and said, They have chickens there, and in calling the chickens they say, *Chik chik chik*. They have cows also, and very often the cows holler, *Moo moo moo.*

She was very angry about these remarks of the silly woman. She was remembering the old country and the old life, and I knew she would take up the story of her husband Melik in no time and begin to shout, so I sat up and smiled at her.

Is that all she had to say? I said. *Chik chik chik* and *moo moo moo?*

She was foolish, said my grandmother. I guess that's why they sent her to school and taught her to read and write. Finally she married a man who was crippled in the left leg. One cripple deserves another, she said. Why aren't you walking in the park on a day like this?

I thought I'd have a little afternoon nap, I said.

For the love of God, said my grandmother, my husband Melik was a man who rode a black horse through the hills and forests all day and half the night, drinking and singing. When the townspeople saw him coming they would run and hide. The wild Kourds of the desert trembled in his presence. I am ashamed of you, she said, lolling around among these silly books.

She lifted the first book that came to her hand, opened it, and stared with disgust at the print.

What is all this language here? she said.

That's a very great book by a very great man, I said. Dostoyevsky he was called. He was a Russian.

Don't tell me about the Russians, said my grandmother. What tricks they played on us. What does he say here?

Everything, I said. He says we must love our neighbors and be kind to the weak.

More lies, said my grandmother. Which tribe of the earth was kind to our tribe? In the dead of winter he went to Stamboul.

Who? I said.

Melik, she shouted. My own husband, she said bitterly. Who else? Who else would dare to go that far in the dead of winter? I will bring you a bright shawl from Stamboul, hc said. I will bring you a bracelet and a necklace. He was drunk of course, but he was my husband. I bore him seven children before he was killed. There would have been more if he hadn't been killed, she groaned.

I have heard he was a cruel man, I said.

Who said such an unkind thing about my husband? said my grandmother. He was impatient with fools and weaklings, she said. You should try to be like this man.

I could use a horse all right, I said. I like drinking and singing too.

In this country? said my grandmother. Where could you go with a horse in this country?

I could go to the public library with a horse, I said.

And they'd lock you in jail, she said. Where would you tie the horse?

I would tie the horse to a tree, I said. There are six small trees in front of the public library.

Ride a horse in this country, she said, and they will put you down for a maniac.

They have already, I said. The libel is spreading like wildfire.

You don't care? she said.

Not at all, I said. Why should I?

Is it true, perhaps? she said.

It is a foul lie, I said.

It is healthful to be disliked, said my grandmother. My husband Melik was hated by friend and enemy alike. *Bitterly* hated, and he knew it, and yet everybody pretended to like him. They were afraid of him, so they pretended to like him. Will you play a game of *scambile?* I have the cards.

She was lonely again, like a young girl.

I got up and sat across the table from her and lit a cigarette for her and one for myself. She shuffled and dealt three cards to me and three to herself and turned over the next card, and the game began.

Ten cents? she said.

Ten or fifteen, I said.

Fifteen then, but I play a much better game than you, she said.

I may be lucky, I said.

I do not believe in luck, she said, not even in card games. I believe in thinking and knowing what you are doing.

We talked and played and I lost three games to my grandmother. I paid her, only I gave her a half-dollar.

Is that what it comes to? she said.

It comes to a little less, I said.

You are not lying? she said.

I never lie, I said. It comes to forty-five cents. You owe me five cents.

Five pennies? she said.

Or one nickel, I said.

I have three pennies, she said. I will pay you three pennies now and owe you two.

Your arithmetic is improving, I said.

American money confuses me, she said, but you never heard of anyone cheating me, did you?

Never, I admitted.

They don't dare, she said. I count the money piece by piece, and if someone is near by I have him count it for me too. There was this thief of a grocer in Hanford, she said. Dikranian. Three cents more he took. Six pounds of cheese. I had five different people count for me. Three cents more he has taken, they said. I waited a week and then went to his store again. For those three cents I took three packages of cigarettes. From a thief thieve and God will smile on you. I never enjoyed cigarettes as much as those I took from Dikranian. Five people counted for me. He thought I was an old woman. He thought he could do such a thing. I went back to the store and said not a word. Good morning, good morning. Lovely day, lovely day. A pound of rice, a pound of rice. He turned to get the rice, I took three packages of cigarettes.

Ha ha, said my grandmother. From thief thieve, and from above God will smile.

But you took too much, I said. You took fifteen times too much.

Fifteen times too much? said my grandmother. He took three pennies, I took three packages of cigarettes, no more, no less.

Well, I said, it probably comes to the same thing anyway,

but you don't really believe God smiles when you steal from a thief, do you?

Of course I believe, said my grandmother. Isn't it said in three different languages, Armenian, Kourdish, and Turkish?

She said the words in Kourdish and Turkish.

I wish I knew how to talk those languages, I said.

Kourdish, said my grandmother, is the language of the heart. Turkish is music. Turkish flows like a stream of wine, smooth and sweet and bright in color. Our tongue, she shouted, is a tongue of bitterness. We have tasted much of death and our tongue is heavy with hatred and anger. I have heard only one man who could speak our language as if it were the tongue of a God-like people.

Who was that man? I asked.

Melik, said my grandmother. My husband Melik. If he was sober, he spoke quietly, his voice rich and deep and gentle, and if he was drunk, he roared like a lion and you'd think God in Heaven was crying lamentations and oaths upon the tribes of the earth. No other man have I heard who could speak in this way, drunk or sober, not one, here or in the old country.

And when he laughed? I said.

When Melik laughed, said my grandmother, it was like an ocean of clear water leaping at the moon with delight.

I tell you, my grandmother would walk away with every silver loving cup and gold ribbon in the world.

Now she was angry, ferocious with the tragic poetry of her race.

And not one of you *opegh-tsapegh* brats are like him, she shouted. Only my son Vahan is a little like him, and after Vahan all the rest of you are strangers to me. This is my greatest grief.

Opegh-tsapegh is untranslatable. It means, somewhat, *very haphazardly assembled,* and when said of someone, it means he is no particular credit to the race of man. On the contrary, only another fool, someone to include in the census and forget. In short, everybody.

And when he cried? I said.

My husband was never known to weep, said my grandmother. When other men hid themselves in their houses and frightened their wives and children by weeping, my husband rode into the hills, drunk and cursing. If he wept in the hills, he wept alone, with only God to witness his weakness. He always came back, though, swearing louder than ever, and then I would put him to bed and sit over him, watching his face.

She sat down with a sigh and again stared bitterly around the room.

These books, she said. I don't know what you expect to learn from books. What is in them? What do you expect to learn from reading?

I myself sometimes wonder, I said.

You have read them all? she said.

Some twice, some three times, I said. Some only a page here and there.

And what is their message?

Nothing much, I said. Sometimes there is brightness and laughter, or maybe the opposite, gloom and anger. Not often, though.

Well, said my grandmother, the ones who were taught to read and write were always the silliest and they made the worst wives. This soft-brained Oskan went to school, and when she got up to speak all she could say was, They have chickens there, and in calling the chickens they say, *Chik chik chik.* Is that wisdom?

That's innocence, I said in English.

I cannot understand such an absurd language, she said.

It is a splendid language, I said.

That is because you were born here and can speak no other language, no Turkish, no Kourdish, not one word of Arabic.

No, I said, it is because this is the language Shakespeare spoke and wrote.

Shakespeare? said my grandmother. Who is he?

He is the greatest poet the world has ever known, I said.

Nonsense, said my grandmother. There was a travelling minstrel who came to our city when I was a girl of twelve. This man was as ugly as Satan, but he could recite poetry in six different languages, all day and all night, and not one word of it written, not one word of it memorized, every line of it made up while he stood before the people, reciting. They called him Crazy Markos and people gave him small coins for reciting and the more coins they gave him the drunker he got and the drunker he got the more beautiful the poems he recited.

Well, I said, each country and race and time has its own kind of poet and its own understanding of poetry. The English poets wrote and your poets recited.

But if they were poets, said my grandmother, why did they write? A poet lives to sing. Were they afraid a good thing would be lost and forgotten? Why do they write each of their thoughts? Are they afraid something will be lost?

I guess so, I said.

Do you want something to eat? said my grandmother. I have cabbage soup and bread.

I'm not hungry, I said.

Are you going out again tonight? she said.

Yes, I said. There is an important meeting of philosophers in the city tonight. I have been invited to listen and learn.

Why don't you stop all this nonsense? she said.

This isn't nonsense, I said. These philosophers are going to explain how we can make this world a better place, a heaven on earth.

It *is* nonsense, said my grandmother. This place is the same place all men have known, and it is anything you like.

That's bourgeois talk, I said in English.

These philosophers, I said in Armenian, are worrying about the poor. They want the wealth of the rich to be shared with the poor. That way they claim everything will be straightened out and everybody will be happy.

Everybody is poor, said my grandmother. The richest man in the world is no less poor than the poorest. All over the world there is poverty of spirit. I never saw such miserliness in people. Give them all the money in the world and they'll still be poor. That's something between themselves and God.

They don't believe in God, I said.

Whether they believe or not, said my grandmother, it is still a matter between themselves and God. I don't believe in evil, but does that mean evil does not exist?

Well, I said, I'm going anyway, just to hear what they have to say.

Then I must be in the house alone? she said.

Go to a movie, I said. You know how to get to the neighborhood theater. It's not far. There is a nice picture tonight.

Alone? said my grandmother. I wouldn't think of it.

Tomorrow, I said, we will go together. Tonight you can listen to the radio. I will come home early.

Have you no books with pictures?

Of course, I said.

I handed her a book called *The Life of Queen Victoria,* full of pictures of that nice old lady.

You will like this lady, I said. She was Queen of England,

but she is now dead. The book is full of pictures, from birth to death.

Ah, said my grandmother looking at an early picture of the Queen. She was a beautiful girl. Ahkh, ahkh, alas, alas, for the good who are dead, and my grandmother went down the hall to the kitchen.

I got out of my old clothes and jumped under a warm shower. The water was refreshing to the skin and I began to sing.

I put on fresh clothes and a dark suit. I went into the kitchen and kissed my grandmother's hand, then left the house. She stood at the front window, looking down at me.

Then she lifted the window and stuck her head out.

Boy, she shouted. Don't be so serious. Get a little drunk.

O.K., I said.

III

Now, a man's life begins from the beginning, every moment he is alive, wakeful or not, conscious or not, and the beginning is as distant in the past as the ending is in the future, and walking to town, alive and miraculously out of pain, I looked upon the world and remembered. Sometimes, even in the artificial and fantastic world we have made, we are able somehow to reach a state of *being* in which pain does not exist and for the moment seems forever an unreality. Miraculously out of pain, I say, because in this place, in this configuration of objects and ideas which we call the world, pain in the living seems more reasonable than the absence of pain, and the reason is this: that *stress* (and not ease) is the basic scheme of function in our life, in this world. All things, even the most simple, require effort in order to be performed, and to me this is an unnatural state of affairs.

And I do not mean sloth. I mean ease and effortlessness. Grace. Which all living creatures, save man, naturally possess, the bird, the fish, the cat, the reptile. I mean inward grace, inherent freedom of form, inherent truthfulness of being.

I mean, *being,* but in this world ease and truthfulness are difficult because of the multitude of encumbrances halting the body and spirit of man on all sides: the heavy and tortuous ideas of civilization, the entanglement of the actual world in which we are born and from which we seem never to be able to emerge, and, above all things, our imprisonment in the million errors of the past, some noble, some half-glorious, some half-godly, but most of them vicious and weak and sorrowful.

We know we are caught in this tragic entanglement, and all that we do is full of the unholiness of this heritage of errors, and all that we do is painful and difficult, even unto the simplest function of living creatures, even unto mere being, mere breathing, mere growing, and our suffering is eternally intensified by impatience, dissatisfaction, and that dreadful hope which is all but maddening in that its fulfillment seems unlikely, our hope for liberation, for sudden innocent and unencumbered reality, sudden and unending naturalness of movement, sudden godliness.

So we turn, somewhat in despair, to the visible in our problem, to matter, and we say if all men had food enough to eat, shelter and comfort, once again all would be well in the world and man would regain the truthfulness of his nature and be joyous.

Anyway, I was walking to town, whistling a comical American song, at five in the afternoon, feeling for a moment altogether truthful and unencumbered, feeling, in short, somewhat happy, personally, when suddenly and apparently for no reason, at least no *new* reason, the whole world, caught in time and space, seemed to me an absurdity, an insanity, and instead of being amused, which would have been philosophical, I was miserable and began to ridicule all the tragic straining of man, living and dead.

I guess I'd better get drunk at that, I said, but this, of all evasions, is the most comic and tragic, since one escapes to nowhere, or at any rate to a universe even more disorderly, if more magnificent, than our own, and then returns with sickened senses and a stunned spirit to the place only recently forsaken.

The drunkard is the most absurd of the individualists, the ultimate egoist, who rises and falls in no domain other than that of his own senses, though drunkards have been, and will long be, most nearly the children of God, most truthfully worshippers of the universal.

I began to feel down in the mouth. I began to feel lousy, or, as my grandmother would say in Armenian, melancholy, which is my natural state, except when I am among others and then my natural state is this: to oppose possible error with possible laughter, since laughter, though largely pointless, is at least less damaging than error, and less pompous than blind sincerity, which is infinitely more dangerous than utter irresponsibility. In fact, I admire most those men of wisdom who accept the tragic obligation to be irresponsible until the time when sincerity will have become natural and noble and not artificial and vicious as it is now.

I walked to The Barrel House on Third Street, the street in San Francisco where the misery of man stalks back and forth in the nightmare images of creatures once mortal.

And I stood in the street, clean and comfortable and secure and out of danger, and angry with myself and with the world that had done these things to these men, asking myself what I intended to do about it. The thick smell of fear in the air, of decay, the decay of flesh, of spirit, the waste of animal energy mingling with the rotten smells pouring out of the doorways and windows of the cheap restaurants, and I said, Breathe deeply, draw deeply into your lungs the odor of the death of man, of man alive, yet dead, most filthily dead, yet alive, and let the foul air of this death feed your blood, and let this death be your death, for these men are your brothers, each of these men is yourself, and when they die, you die, and if they cannot live, you cannot live, though you forsake the world and enter a world of your own, you die.

And what will you do about this? Here is one who may be saved. A boy, years younger than yourself, young enough to be saved. And this old man who is crippled, whose face is the mask of one in hell, yet on earth, what are you going to do about him?

Be a gentleman and give him a dime for coffee and doughnuts. Humiliate him again and let his trembling hand close upon the small coin, his rotted heart close upon the cheap charity of the strong and secure, and the old man went by, and across the street the shabby saints of the Salvation Army preached and prayed and sang and asked the hungry men for alms with which to spread the holy gospel of truth, and the men gave no alms.

When the revolution comes, these men will be like gods, and their sons will come into the earth innocent and whole, and within them will be no germ of sin, no germ of greed or envy or cruelty or hatred, and they will grow to be greater gods than their fathers, and the daughters of these dead men will move upon the earth with the feline power and grace and poise of jungle cats, and when the revolution comes all misery on earth will end, and all error will end.

Indeed. And the thing to do is to get cockeyed, to be blind and deaf, to go stumbling through the filth of the world, laughing and singing.

I walked into The Barrel House and sat at a table.

Nicora, the waiter, came over and wiped the table clean, leaving the wood moist, standing sullenly, a little drunk, his dark Italian face weary and worried, yet indifferent, lots of trouble in the world, *paesano,* but I got a good job: all day I drink, what do I care about trouble? Wife, two kids, and himself, and when the revolution comes Nicora will serve drinks to his brothers in a big garden in the sun.

Hi-ya, Nick, I said.

O.K., kid, he said. Little shot, maybe?

Yeah, I said. How's your wife?

Oh fine, he said. She's very sick, another kid coming.

Congratulations, I said, and he went to the bar and got a drink.

He put it down in front of me, talking.

I tell you, kid, he said, take my advice, don't get married, first the wife, then the kids, then the rent, then the bread, then the kid falls down and breaks the arm, then the wife cries, then you get drunk, then the wife's brother comes and makes trouble, then you fight him, then the jail, then you sit inside the jail and think, and Jesus Christ, kid, don't be crazy and get married, I know, and I don't want to see another guy in trouble.

All right, Nick, I said.

I swallowed the whisky and it burned all the way down and I began to feel all right, like a big gesture in the world, all right, and I began to feel gay and at the same time very proud, like, *who, me?*

Don't worry about me, pals, just worry about yourselves: I'm doing all right, pals, and I told Nick to get me another because I figured I'd get good and drunk and laugh the way my grandfather Melik used to laugh when he got drunk in the old country, and Nick brought another and I swallowed it, and I told him to get another and he did and I swallowed this one, everything's O.K., pals, and another, and then I started to laugh, but not out loud, only inside, away back in the old country, on the black horse, riding through the hills, in the beginning, cussing and singing.

IV

Drink expands the eye, enlarges the inward vision, elevates the ego. The eye perceives less and less the objects of this world and more and more the objects and patterns and rhythms of the other: the large and limitless and magnificent universe of remembrance, the real and timeless earth of history, of man's legend in this place. Until, of course, one is under the table. Then the magnificence is succeeded by sensory riot and lawlessness, and the law of gravity comes to an end, amid comedy and tragedy. Distance is unreal, and flesh and spirit exist not alone in one place and in one time but in all places and during all times, including the future. In short, one achieves the ridiculous and glorious state of fool.

The gesture blossoms in the universe, dramatic and significant, saying I *know*, the language of limb in motion, artfully. The head wags yea and nay. The tongue loosens with the chaos of a million languages. The spirit laughs and the flesh leaps, and sitting at a small table in a dark saloon, one travels somehow to all places of the world, returns, and goes again, gesturing and reciting, wagging the head and laughing, singing and leaping.

I got a little drunk sitting at the small table, and Nicora came and went, telling me what to do and what not to do in order to be happy in the world, my spiritual adviser.

I wished Paula were getting drunk with me, sitting across the table from me, so I could see her round white face with the deep melancholy eyes and the full melancholy lips and the pert melancholy nose and the small melancholy ears and the brown melancholy hair, and I wished I could take her warm melancholy hand and walk with her over the hard melancholy streets of our dark melancholy city and reach a large melancholy room with a good melancholy bed and lie with her beautiful melancholy body, and all during the night have a quiet melancholy conversation between long melancholy embraces and in the morning waken from deep melancholy sleep and hide our cold melancholy nakedness with cheap melancholy clothes and go out for a big cheerful breakfast.

So I went to the telephone booth and dropped a nickel in the slot and dialed the number. I guess I dialed the wrong number or forgot the right one because the girl who answered wasn't Paula. She didn't have Paula's quiet melancholy voice: she had a loud melancholy voice.

This is fate, I said, or something like it, so I talked to the girl. The telephone is a great invention. If you get a wrong number, it doesn't make much difference because you get a girl anyway, even if it isn't the one you had in mind, and the whole thing amounts to fate, slightly assisted by the noble mechanics of our age.

What's the good of getting a wrong number if you don't talk a little? Where's the Christian kindliness and love of neighbor in hanging up on a girl with a loud melancholy voice just because you've never seen her?

Young lady, I said, I'm getting drunk on rotten whiskey at The Barrel House on Third Street. Jump into the first streetcar and come right down and have a drink. After a while we will take a taxi to The Universe Restaurant on Columbus Avenue and have a dinner of spaghetti and roast chicken. We will sit at the table and talk and we will go through the city and see the sights. When we are tired we will go to a movie or if you prefer we will go to a Communist meeting and join our comrades in singing the Internationale and in hating the guts of the rich.

The girl hung up with a fierce melancholy bang. I dialed the number again and the bell rang once, twice, three times, four times, and then it was Paula.

Hello, said Paula.

Hello, I said.

How are you? said Paula.

I'm fine, I said. How are you?

Fine, said Paula. What's the matter?

Nothing, I said. Something the matter?

You sound serious, said Paula.

Wait a minute, I said. I want to light a cigarette.

All right, said Paula. I want to light one too.

I inhaled smoke and began to feel less and less gay.

Hello, I said.

Hello, said Paula.

I heard her exhale smoke, and even this sounded melancholy. I could see her round melancholy face.

How are you, Paula? I said.

I'm fine, Mike, she said. How are you, Mike?

I'm fine too, I said.

I guess we both feel lousy, said Paula.

No, I said. I feel great.

I went to a movie last night, said Paula.

How was it? I said.

Great, said Paula. It was just like life.

Did you cry? I said.

No, said Paula, I laughed. It was about a boy and a girl in love. A new idea in the movies. They had a lot of trouble at first, but in the end they were married.

Then what happened? I said.

The movie ended, said Paula.

That's bourgeois propaganda, I said. I saw a movie like that once. They got married too.

Must have been the same boy and girl, said Paula.

The universal male and female, I said.

Then I got sore at myself for being smart again. I wasn't saying what I wanted to say the way I wanted to say it, and I got sore.

Listen, Paula, I said, to hell with that stuff.

Sure, said Paula. To hell with it.

Paula, I said, come to town and have dinner with me.

Can't, said Paula. I'm going out.

Who with? I said.

Friend of mine, said Paula.

Sure, but who? I said.

Young lawyer, said Paula. You don't know him.

Tell him you're sick, I said, and come to town and have dinner with me.

Can't, said Paula.

What the hell you talking about? I said.

We're going to be married, said Paula. Just like in the movies.

You're kidding, I said.

Look in next Sunday's *Examiner,* said Paula. My picture, his name.

Jesus Christ, I said.

I'm in love with him, said Paula.

Sure, I said. You sound *madly* in love. You're crazy.

Listen, Paula, I said. I want to see you tonight. Go ahead and get married. I don't care about that. But I want to see you tonight. What time will you be through with the young lawyer?

You can't, said Paula.

You're crazy, I said.

Maybe, and maybe not, said Paula. I'll know after a while.

Oh I see, I said.

I'd like to meet the lawyer, I said.

You can't, said Paula.

Oh, I said.

We didn't talk for half a minute.

O.K., Paula, I said. I'll see you by accident in the street sometime.

Sure, said Paula. It's a small world. So long, Mike.

So long, Paula, I said.

I went back to the small table and Nick began bringing me drinks again. The more I drank the worse I felt. When I went outside it was raining. The rain was fine, and the air was clear and good. I walked through the wet melancholy streets to the Reno Club on Geary Street. I walked in and there was a seat open in a draw poker game, so I sat down. I'm pretty lucky when I'm a little drunk. Apostolos, the Greek restaurant man, dealt the cards. I played two hours and came out four dollars ahead.

Then I went up to Fillmore Street to the Communist meeting, and began climbing the stairs.

I'm drunk, I said, and Paula's getting married to a lawyer, and Pete wants to save the world, and my grandmother is homesick for Armenia, and Nick's wife is going to have another baby, and listen, comrades, if I don't go easy climbing these stairs I'll fall down and bust my head, comrades. What good will it do when everybody has bread, comrades, what good will it do when everybody has cake, comrades, what good will it do when everybody has everything, comrades, everything isn't enough, comrades, and the living aren't alive, brothers, the living are dead, brothers, even the living are not alive, brothers, and you can't ever do anything about that.

Our Friends the Mice

In spite of our cat, there were mice in our house. At night when it was very quiet and the lights were out and we were in our beds we could hear the mice coming out of their holes and running over the wood floor of our kitchen, and if we listened carefully we could hear them squeak, and it was amusing to listen to them. I thought it was very good to have these small timid and secretive things in our house, and I thought of them as being our mice, the mice of our house, and therefore I felt that they were a part of our life. They were thieves and they had to steal their food, but all the same they were a family, just as we were a family, and since they were living in our house with us I had affection for them.

Sometimes at night, listening to the mice, I could feel my brother Krikor listening to them with me. We slept in the same room and his bed was beside mine so that we were very close, and if I was awake in the darkness and he was awake I could *feel* that he was awake because it was different when he was asleep. I could feel him listening to the mice with me, and I would say, Do you hear them, Krikor? And Krikor would say, Don't talk. They will start to play now. I could feel that he was awake because there would be something of his wakefulness in the darkness, and it would not be there if he was asleep; so that listening to the mice we came quietly to the realization of our own sustained reality, the moment to moment reality of our consciousness which could rest in sleep but would always return with wakefulness, and except for the mice in our house we might not have come to this realization so quickly and by so simple a device.

Moog, the word for mouse in our language, is not scientific in implication, but signifies a small form of life which possesses alertness and is easily frightened, and if a child is small and shy, he may be affectionately called by this name. Thinking of our mice in our language we thought of timidity and playfulness, and not of disease, and we did not feel that the mice in our house were the enemies of our health and the thieves of our pantry. They did do a little innocent nibbling here and there, and sometimes we found their waste on our floor, but this was the worst we could say of them. None of us got malaria because of the mice, and Krikor, when we spoke of the matter, said that if the mice had malaria they themselves would probably die before they ever got the germs to us. He was unscientific also.

Only once or twice had we seen our cat with a mouse it had caught. We had seen how the cat played with a mouse and finally ate the mouse, and while it was rather startling to understand that something living was being deprived of its life, and while the sound of the small bones being broken made us feel sad, the performance struck us as being proper because it was legitimate. Cats were fond of eating mice, and it was part of the mouse's business to keep out of the way of cats. A cat was a living thing like a mouse, only of another family and on another scale, and they both had natural wits, and it was natural for a cat to use its wits to try to catch mice, and it was natural for a mouse to use its wits to keep out of the way of cats. The whole situation was honorable and decent, and if a mouse fell into the paws of a cat, it was due either to the fact that the cat, owing to hunger or longing for play, had exercised a special degree of craftiness, or to the fact that the mouse, owing to age or downright negligence, had not exercised sufficient caution, and therefore the cat deserved to eat the mouse, and the mouse deserved to die.

There is hardly any other satisfactory viewpoint, and it is pointless to sympathize with the mice and to feel that cats are unlovely and savage things or that they have in any way the advantage, because, if anything, the odds are against them, and if you will stop to think about the matter you will wonder how a cat is ever able to catch a mouse. To sympathize with the mouse is utterly unfair and narrow, and indicates a very poor perception of the laws of nature, and the ethics of being a mouse or a cat. I am not a naturalist, and I do not know the names of the smaller living things mice prey upon and eat, but I suppose they prey upon and eat some sort of small living things. If they do not, however, and if they eat only the food men eat, cheese and first editions, then they ought to be even more admired than they already are.

I had seen mouse-traps before, but I had never studied one closely, and I had certainly never thought of one in relation to *our* mice. Now we had these three mouse-traps and my sister Lucy was determined to rid our house of the mice. I held one of the traps in my hand and I looked at it closely. I saw clearly the strong wire that would snap down over the mouse and crush it to death, and I saw the wire that was wound into a spring that would bring the wire down with a terrific force. When a cat has a mouse and is playing with it, it is not hard to imagine the mouse's hectic inward state, its amazement, its horror, its tragic hope for escape, which the cat so cruelly encourages in order to be amused, but in spite of all these things, as I have said, one has a feeling that the whole business is proper. It is impossible to have this feeling about traps. A metal spring and a mouse's instinctive wit are hardly a fair match.

I was opposed to the mouse-traps at the outset, and I was amazed that my brother Krikor had no objection to make. He looked at the traps and did not bother to make any sort of a remark, one way or another. I said in Armenian, What have the mice done? They haven't done anything. My mother said she had found a mouse drowned in a jug of vinegar and that she had had to pour the vinegar down the sink. She said it was absurd to tolerate the mice simply because we liked to hear them at night.

Cheese was placed in the mouse-traps and they were set, and in the morning we found that two of them had caught mice but that one of them had become unset and did not have a mouse in it. The cheese was gone. My mother thought this was very strange. It must have been a very shrewd mouse, she said. I felt very happy because one of our mice had got away alive, and I had an idea this mouse returned to the other mice and said, They've got traps up there now with cheese in them. You go to get the cheese and something comes down over you and kills you. I saw it happen and it nearly happened to me, but I was too quick for it. I want you to be very careful from now on and I want you to keep your eyes open, and don't be fooled by cheese that isn't where it belongs, on a dish or on a shelf. If you see any wire on a piece of wood, stay away from it. It's a trap. It will kill you. It is better to go hungry and be alive than to get a little piece of cheese in your mouth and then be killed.

The mice that had been killed were stiff and it was possible to tell from their limbs how much they had been pained before they had died. In the evening my sister Lucy placed cheese in the three traps again, and the next morning we found that one of the traps had a mouse in it, while the other two had become unset and did not have mice in them. I felt that our mice were learning very quickly and I was greatly pleased.

Sometime during the following night I became awake and began to listen for the mice. I listened for a little while and I heard nothing and I could feel that my brother Krikor was not awake. Then I heard a trap snap and I began to think about the mouse that was being crushed to death. In less than a minute I heard another trap snap. I wondered what had come over the mice. Why hadn't they learned to stay away from traps? Then I heard the third trap snap, and I thought, Well, at this rate, all our mice will be killed in less than a week. And I fell asleep.

In the morning we found that all of the traps had become unset, but that not one of them had caught a mouse. At the breakfast table my brother Krikor said, I read in a book that some mice understand about traps and won't be fooled. They go up around the back way where the spring doesn't work and they eat the cheese and go away. Our mice are doing this.

Well, it was my brother Krikor. After a while he came back to our room and got in bed. I was so wide-awake by this time and I was thinking so steadily about the traps and our mice that my brother Krikor found out about my being awake. We began to whisper softly and my brother Krikor said, I went to fix the traps. We don't want to kill those mice with traps. I put the cheese on the floor for them and they will come pretty soon and eat it and go away. We will hear them when they come.

And we began to listen for the mice, and after a while we heard them coming out of their holes, and my brother Krikor said, It is not true about the germs. They are as clean as a cat. Only they have hunger like anything else alive. I put the cheese by the hole and they will find it.

The Man with the Heart in the Highlands

In 1914, when I was not quite six years old, an old man came down San Benito Avenue playing a solo on a bugle and stopped in front of our house. I ran out of the yard and stood at the curb waiting for him to start playing again, but he wouldn't do it. I said, I sure would like to hear you play another tune, and he said, Young man, could you get a glass of water for an old man whose heart is not here, but in the highlands?

What highlands? I said.

The Scotch highlands, said the old man. Could you?

What's your heart doing in the Scotch highlands? I said.

My heart is grieving there, said the old man. Could you bring me a glass of cool water?

Where's your mother? I said.

My mother's in Tulsa, Oklahoma, said the old man, but her heart isn't.

Where *is* her heart? I said.

In the Scotch highlands, said the old man. I am very thirsty, young man.

How come the members of your family are always leaving their hearts in the highlands? I said.

That's the way we are, said the old man. Here today and gone tomorrow.

Here today and gone tomorrow? I said. How do you figure?

Alive one minute and dead the next, said the old man.

Where is your mother's *mother?* I said.

She's up in Vermont, in a little town called White River, but her heart isn't, said the old man.

Is her poor old withered heart in the highlands too? I said.

Right smack in the highlands, said the old man. Son, I'm dying of thirst.

My father came out on the porch and roared like a lion that has just awakened from evil dreams.

Johnny, he roared, get the hell away from that poor old man. Get him a pitcher of water before he falls down and dies. Where in hell are your manners?

Can't a fellow try to find out something from a traveler once in a while? I said.

Get the old gentleman some water, said my father. God damn it, don't stand there like a dummy. Get him a drink before he falls down and dies.

You get him a drink, I said. You ain't doing nothing.

Ain't doing nothing? said my father. Why, Johnny, you know God damn well I'm getting a new poem arranged in my mind.

How do you figure I know? I said. You're just standing there on the porch with your sleeves rolled up. How do you figure I know?

Well, you ought to know, said my father.

Good afternoon, said the old man to my father. Your son has been telling me how clear and cool the climate is in these parts.

(Jesus Christ, I said, I never did tell this old man anything about the climate. Where's he getting that stuff from?)

Good afternoon, said my father. Won't you come in for a little rest? We should be honored to have you at our table for a bit of lunch.

Sir, said the old man, I am starving. I shall come right in.

Can you play *Drink to Me Only with Thine Eyes?* I said to the old man. I sure would like to hear you play that song on the bugle. That song is my favorite. I guess I like that song better than any other song in the world.

Son, said the old man, when you get to be my age you'll know songs aren't important, bread is the thing.

Anyway, I said, I sure would like to hear you play that song.

The old man went up on the porch and shook hands with my father.

My name is Jasper MacGregor, he said. I am an actor.

I am mighty glad to make your acquaintance, said my father. Johnny, get Mr. MacGregor a pitcher of water.

I went around to the well and poured some cool water into a pitcher and took it to the old man. He drank the whole pitcherful in one long swig. Then he looked around at the landscape and up at the sky and away up San Benito Avenue where the evening sun was beginning to go down.

I reckon I'm five thousand miles from home, he said. Do you think we could eat a little bread and cheese to keep my body and spirit together?

Johnny, said my father, run down to the grocer's and get a loaf of French bread and a pound of cheese.

Give me the money, I said.

Tell Mr. Kosak to give us credit, said my father. I ain't got a penny, Johnny.

He won't give us credit, I said. Mr. Kosak is tired of giving us credit. He's sore at us. He says we don't work and never pay our bills. We owe him forty cents.

Go on down there and argue it out with him, said my father. You know that's your job.

He won't listen to reason, I said. Mr. Kosak says he doesn't know anything about anything, all he wants is the forty cents.

Go on down there and make him give you a loaf of bread and a pound of cheese, said my father. You can do it, Johnny.

Go on down there, said the old man, and tell Mr. Kosak to give you a loaf of bread and a pound of cheese, son.

Go ahead, Johnny, said my father. You haven't yet failed to leave that store with provender, and you'll be back here in ten minutes with food fit for a king.

I don't know, I said. Mr. Kosak says we are trying to give him the merry run around. He wants to know what kind of work you are doing.

Well, go ahead and tell him, said my father. I have nothing to conceal. I am writing poetry. Tell Mr. Kosak I am writing poetry night and day.

Well, all right, I said, but I don't think he'll be much impressed. He says you never go out like other unemployed men and look for work. He says you're lazy and no good.

You go on down there and tell him he's crazy, Johnny, said my father. You go down there and tell that fellow your father is one of the greatest unknown poets living.

He might not care, I said, but I'll go. I'll do my best. Ain't we got nothing in the house?

Only popcorn, said my father. We been eating popcorn four days in a row now, Johnny. You got to get bread and cheese if you expect me to finish that long poem.

I'll do my best, I said.

Don't take too long, said Mr. MacGregor. I'm five thousand miles from home.

I'll run all the way, I said.

If you find any money on the way, said my father, remember we go fifty-fifty.

All right, I said.

I ran all the way to Mr. Kosak's store, but I didn't find any money on the way, not even a penny.

I went into the store and Mr. Kosak opened his eyes.

Mr. Kosak, I said, if you were in China and didn't have a friend in the world and no money, you'd expect some Christian over there to give you a pound of rice, wouldn't you?

What do you want? said Mr. Kosak.

I just want to talk a little, I said. You'd expect some member of the Aryan race to help you out a little, wouldn't you, Mr. Kosak?

How much money you got? said Mr. Kosak.

It ain't a question of money, Mr. Kosak, I said. I'm talking about being in China and needing the help of the white race.

I don't know nothing about nothing, said Mr. Kosak.

How would you feel in China that way? I said.

I don't know, said Mr. Kosak. What would I be doing in China?

Well, I said, you'd be visiting there, and you'd be hungry, and not a friend in the world. You wouldn't expect a good Christian to turn you away without even a pound of rice, would you, Mr. Kosak?

I guess not, said Mr. Kosak, but you ain't in China, Johnny, and neither is your Pa. You or your Pa's got to go out and work sometime in your lives, so you might as well start now. I ain't going to give you no more groceries on credit because I know you won't pay me.

Mr. Kosak, I said, you misunderstand me: I'm not talking about a few groceries. I'm talking about all them heathen people around you in China, and you hungry and dying.

This ain't China, said Mr. Kosak. You got to go out and make your living in this country. Everybody works in America.

Mr. Kosak, I said, suppose it was a loaf of French bread and a pound of cheese you needed to keep you alive in the world, would you hesitate to ask a Christian missionary for these things?

Yes, I would, said Mr. Kosak. I would be ashamed to ask.

Even if you knew you would give him back two loaves of bread and two pounds of cheese? I said. Even then?

Even then, said Mr. Kosak.

Don't be that way, Mr. Kosak, I said. That's defeatist talk, and you know it. Why, the only thing that would happen to you would be death. You would die out there in China, Mr. Kosak.

I wouldn't care if I would, said Mr. Kosak, you and your Pa have got to pay for bread and cheese. Why don't your Pa go out and get a job?

Mr. Kosak, I said, how are you, anyway?

I'm fine, Johnny, said Mr. Kosak. How are you?

Couldn't be better, Mr. Kosak, I said. How are the children?

Fine, said Mr. Kosak. Stepan is beginning to walk now.

That's great, I said. How is Angela?

Angela is beginning to sing, said Mr. Kosak. How is your grandmother?

She's feeling fine, I said. She's beginning to sing too. She says she would rather be an opera star than queen. How's Marta, your wife, Mr. Kosak?

Oh, swell, said Mr. Kosak.

I cannot tell you how glad I am to hear that all is well at your house, I said. I know Stepan is going to be a great man some day.

I hope so, said Mr. Kosak. I am going to send him straight through high school and see that he gets every chance I didn't get. I don't want him to open a grocery store.

I have great faith in Stepan, I said.

What do you want, Johnny? said Mr. Kosak. And how much money you got?

Mr. Kosak, I said, you know I didn't come here to buy anything. You know I enjoy a quiet philosophical chat with you every now and then. Let me have a loaf of French bread and a pound of cheese.

You got to pay cash, Johnny, said Mr. Kosak.

And Esther, I said. How is your beautiful daughter Esther?

Esther is all right, Johnny, said Mr. Kosak, but you got to pay cash. You and your Pa are the worst citizens in this whole county.

I'm glad Esther is all right, Mr. Kosak, I said. Jasper MacGregor is visiting our house. He is a great actor.

I never heard of him, said Mr. Kosak.

And a bottle of beer for Mr. MacGregor, I said.

I can't give you a bottle of beer, said Mr. Kosak.

Certainly you can, I said.

I can't, said Mr. Kosak. I'll let you have one loaf of stale bread, and one pound of cheese, but that's all. What kind of work does your Pa do when he works, Johnny?

My father writes poetry, Mr. Kosak, I said. That's the only work my father does. He is one of the greatest writers of poetry in the world.

When does he get any money? said Mr. Kosak.

He never gets any money, I said. You can't have your cake and eat it.

I don't like that kind of a job, said Mr. Kosak. Why doesn't your Pa work like everybody else, Johnny?

He works harder than everybody else, I said. My father works twice as hard as the average man.

Well, that's fifty-five cents you owe me, Johnny, said Mr. Kosak. I'll let you have some stuff this time, but never again.

Tell Esther I love her, I said.

All right, said Mr. Kosak.

Goodbye, Mr. Kosak, I said.

Goodbye, Johnny, said Mr. Kosak.

I ran back to the house with the loaf of French bread and the pound of cheese.

My father and Mr. MacGregor were in the street waiting to see if I would come back with food. They ran half a block toward me and when they saw that it was food, they waved back to the house where my grandmother was waiting. She ran into the house to set the table.

I knew you'd do it, said my father.

So did I, said Mr. MacGregor.

He says we got to pay him fifty-five cents, I said. He says he ain't going to give us no more stuff on credit.

That's his opinion, said my father. What did you talk about, Johnny?

First I talked about being hungry and at death's door in China, I said, and then I inquired about the family.

How is everyone? said my father.

Fine, I said.

So we all went inside and ate the loaf of bread and the pound of cheese, and each of us drank two or three quarts of water, and after every crumb of bread had disappeared, Mr. MacGregor began to look around the kitchen to see if there wasn't something else to eat.

That green can up there, he said. What's in there, Johnny?

Marbles, I said.

That cupboard, he said. Anything edible in there, Johnny?

Crickets, I said.

That big jar in the corner there, Johnny, he said. What's good in there?

I got a gopher snake in that jar, I said.

Well, said Mr. MacGregor, I could go for a bit of boiled gopher snake in a big way, Johnny.

You can't have that snake, I said.

Why not, Johnny? said Mr. MacGregor. Why the hell not, son? I hear of fine Borneo natives eating snakes and grasshoppers. You ain't got half a dozen fat grasshoppers around, have you, Johnny?

Only four, I said.

Well, trot them out, Johnny, said Mr. MacGregor, and after we have had our fill, I'll play *Drink to Me Only with Thine Eyes* on the bugle for you. I'm mighty hungry, Johnny.

So am I, I said, but you ain't going to kill that snake.

My father sat at the table with his head in his hands, dreaming. My grandmother paced through the house, singing arias from Puccini. As through the streets I wander, she roared in Italian.

How about a little music? said my father. I think the boy would be delighted.

I sure would, Mr. MacGregor, I said.

All right, Johnny, said Mr. MacGregor.

So he got up and began to blow into the bugle and he blew louder than any man ever blew into a bugle and people for miles around heard him and got excited. Eighteen neighbors gathered in front of our house and applauded when Mr. MacGregor finished the solo. My father led Mr. MacGregor out on the porch and said, Good neighbors and friends, I want you to meet Jasper MacGregor, the greatest Shakespearean actor of our day.

The good neighbors and friends said nothing and Mr. MacGregor said, I remember my first appearance in London in 1867 as if it was yesterday, and he went on with the story of his career. Rufe Apley the carpenter said, How about some more music, Mr. MacGregor? and Mr. MacGregor said, Have you got an egg at your house?

I sure have, said Rufe. I got a dozen eggs at my house.

Would it be convenient for you to go and get one of them

dozen eggs? said Mr. MacGregor. When you return I'll play a song that will make your heart leap with joy and grief.

I'm on my way already, said Rufe, and he went home to get an egg.

Mr. MacGregor asked Tom Baker if he had a bit of sausage at his house and Tom said he did, and Mr. MacGregor asked Tom if it would be convenient for Tom to go and get that little bit of sausage and come back with it and when Tom returned Mr. MacGregor would play a song on the bugle that would change the whole history of Tom's life. And Tom went home for the sausage, and Mr. MacGregor asked each of the eighteen good neighbors and friends if he had something small and nice to eat at his home and each man said he did, and each man went to his home to get the small and nice thing to eat, so Mr. MacGregor would play the song he said would be so wonderful to hear, and when all the good neighbors and friends had returned to our house with all the small and nice things to eat, Mr. MacGregor lifted the bugle to his lips and played *My Heart's in the Highlands, My Heart is not Here,* and each of the good neighbors and friends wept and returned to his home, and Mr. MacGregor took all the good things into the kitchen and our family feasted and drank and was merry: an egg, a sausage, a dozen green onions, two kinds of cheese, butter, two kinds of bread, boiled potatoes, fresh tomatoes, a melon, tea, and many other good things to eat, and we ate and our bellies tightened, and Mr. MacGregor said, Sir, if it is all the same to you I should like to dwell in your house for some days to come, and my father said, Sir, my house is your house, and Mr. MacGregor stayed at our house seventeen days and seventeen nights, and on the afternoon of the eighteenth day a man from the Old People's Home came to our house and said, I am looking for Jasper MacGregor, the actor, and my father said, What do you want?

I am from the Old People's Home, said the young man, and I want Mr. MacGregor to come back to our place because we are putting on our annual show in two weeks and need an actor.

Mr. MacGregor got up from the floor where he had been dreaming and went away with the young man, and the following afternoon, when he was very hungry, my father said, Johnny, go down to Mr. Kosak's store and get a little something to eat. I know you can do it, Johnny. Get anything you can.

Mr. Kosak wants fifty-five cents, I said. He won't give us anything more without money.

Go on down there, Johnny, said my father. You know you can get that fine Slovak gentleman to give you a bit of something to eat.

So I went down to Mr. Kosak's store and took up the Chinese problem where I had dropped it, and it was quite a job for me to go away from the store with a box of bird seed and half a can of maple syrup, but I did it, and my father said, Johnny, this sort of fare is going to be pretty dangerous for the old lady, and sure enough in the morning we heard my grandmother singing like a canary, and my father said, How the hell can I write great poetry on bird seed?

The Mexicans

Juan Cabral was a tall Mexican who worked for my uncle, pruning vines. He was a poor man with a number of possessions: his wife Consuela, his sons Pablo and Pancho, his three daughters, his lame cousin Federico, four dogs, a cat, a guitar, a shotgun, an old horse, an old wagon, and lots of pots and pans.

I was in the farmyard talking to my uncle the morning Juan came up the road in his wagon to ask for work.

What's this? my uncle said.

Mexicans, I said.

How can you tell? he said.

The dogs, I said. The Mexicans are a noble and simple people. They are never so poor they cannot keep a pack of hounds. They are Indians, mixed with other noble races.

What do they want? he said.

Work, I said. It will break their hearts to admit it, but that's what they want.

I don't need any help, my uncle said.

They won't care, I said. They'll just turn around and go on to the next vineyard.

The wagon came slowly into the farmyard and Juan Cabral

said good morning in Mexican. *Buenos dias, amigos.* In bad English he said, Is there work on this vineyard for a strong Mexican?

Who? said my uncle. (For instance, he said to me.)

Me, said Juan Cabral. Juan Cabral.

Juan Cabral, said my uncle. No, there is no work.

How much is the pay? said Juan.

What'd he say? said my uncle to me. He lit a cigarette to help him through his bewilderment.

He wants to know how much the pay is, I said.

Who said anything about pay? my uncle said. I'm not hiring anybody.

He wants to know anyway, I said. He knows you're not hiring anybody.

My uncle was amazed.

Well, he said, I'm paying the Japs thirty cents an hour. Most farmers are paying twenty and twenty-five.

The pay is thirty cents an hour, I said to Juan.

That is not enough, said the Mexican. There are many mouths to feed this winter.

What's he say? said my uncle.

My uncle was pretty sore and wouldn't understand anything Juan said until I said it over again.

He says thirty cents an hour isn't enough to feed all the mouths he's got to feed this winter, I said.

Who's he got to feed? my uncle said.

All them people in the wagon, I said.

Where they going to live? my uncle said.

I don't know, I said. They'll find a place somewhere, I suppose.

Juan Cabral did not speak. One of his dogs came over to my uncle and licked my uncle's hand. My uncle jumped and looked around fearfully. What's this? he said.

It's one of the Mexican's dogs, I said.

Well, get it away from me, said my uncle.

I told the dog to go back to the wagon and it did.

My uncle watched it go back. He not only watched the dog go back, he studied the dog going back.

That's an ordinary dog, he said. You see hundreds of them in the streets.

That's right, I said.

That dog ain't worth a penny, my uncle said.

It ain't even worth a lot less than a penny, I said. You couldn't give that dog away with two dollars.

I wouldn't take that dog with three dollars, my uncle said. What can it do? Can it catch a jack rabbit or anything like that?

No, I said.

Can it scare robbers away? said my uncle.

No, I said. It would go out and lick the hands of robbers.

Well, what good is it? my uncle said.

No good at all, I said.

What do they want to keep a lot of dogs like that for? my uncle said.

They're Mexicans, I said. They're simple Mexican people.

I hear Mexicans do a lot of stealing, said my uncle.

They'll take anything that ain't got roots in the earth, I said.

I got thirteen mouths to feed, not counting my own, said Juan. Thirty cents an hour isn't enough.

Thirteen mouths? said my uncle.

He's counting the animals, I said.

I don't suppose he knows how to prune a vine, my uncle said.

Do you know how to prune a grapevine? I said to Juan.

No, señor, he said. I am a soldier.

What'd he say? said my uncle.

He says he's a soldier, I said.

The war's over, my uncle said.

The Mexican brought out his shotgun and was lifting it to his shoulder by way of demonstrating his being a soldier when my uncle noticed what he was fooling with. My uncle jumped behind me.

Tell him to put that gun away, he said. I don't want any Mexican shooting me accidentally. I believe him. I believe he's a soldier. Tell him to put that God damn gun away. He'll shoot me just to prove he's a soldier.

No, he won't, I said.

I don't need any help, my uncle said to Juan Cabral.

Thirty cents an hour is not enough to feed thirteen mouths, not counting my own, said the Mexican.

He put the gun away, and the first thing my uncle knew five young Mexican faces were looking up at him. He almost lost his balance.

Who are these people? he said.

These are the children, I said. Two boys and three girls.

What do they want? said my uncle.

Beans and flour and salt, I said. They don't want much.

Tell them to go away, my uncle said. He don't know how to prune a vine.

Anybody can learn to prune a vine, I said.

He'll ruin my vineyard, my uncle said.

And steal everything that ain't got roots in the earth, I said.

I'm paying ten cents an hour more than most farmers are paying, my uncle said.

He says it ain't enough, I said.

Well, said my uncle, ask him how much *is* enough.

Señor Cabral, I said to the Mexican, will you work for thirty-five cents an hour? My uncle does not need any help, but he likes you.

Have you a dwelling for my family and the animals? said the Mexican.

Yes, I said. It is modest but comfortable.

Is there much work to do? said the Mexican.

Very little, I said.

Is it pleasant work? said the Mexican.

It is pleasant and healthful, I said.

Juan Cabral stepped down from the wagon and came over to my uncle. My uncle was pretty scared. The dogs walked behind the Mexican, and his children were already surrounding my uncle.

Señor, said the Mexican to my uncle, I will work in your vineyard.

I am honored, said my uncle.

He was all mixed up. It was the dogs mostly, but it was also the five Mexican children, and the Mexican's magnificent manners.

It was certainly not the gun. My uncle wouldn't let any power in the world intimidate him.

By three o'clock in the afternoon the Mexicans were established in their little house, and I took Juan Cabral, followed by Pablo and Pancho and his lame cousin Federico, to a vine to teach him how to prune. I explained the reasons for each clip of the shears. To keep the shape of the vine. To keep it strong. To let its fresh branches grow upward toward the sun. And so forth. I moved down the row of vines to the next vine. I handed him the pruning shears and asked if he wouldn't enjoy trying to prune the vine. He was very polite and said it would be a pleasure. He worked thoughtfully and slowly, explaining to his children and his lame cousin, as I had explained to him, the reasons for each clip of the shears. His lame cousin Federico, who was a man of sixty or so, was very much impressed.

I suggested that he go on pruning vines until dark and returned to my uncle who was sitting at the wheel of the Ford, dreaming.

How does it look? he said.

Excellent, I said.

We drove back to the city sixty-six miles an hour, as if my uncle wanted to get away from something frightening, and all the way he didn't speak. When we were coming into Ventura Avenue near the Fair Grounds he said, All four of them dogs ain't worth a penny put together.

It ain't the dogs, I said. Mexicans just look at it that way.

I thought that dog was going to bite me, my uncle said.

No, I said. He wouldn't think of it. Not even if you kicked him. His heart was full of love. The same as the Mexicans. The stealing they do never amounts to anything.

Them kids looked pretty healthy, my uncle said.

They don't come any healthier, I said.

What do they eat? my uncle said.

Beans and Mexican bread, I said. Stuff that ain't supposed to be good for you.

Do you think he'll ever learn to prune a vine? my uncle said.

Sure, I said.

I don't suppose he'll go away with the tractor, will he? my uncle said.

No, I said. It's much too heavy.

I lost money on that vineyard last year, my uncle said.

I know, I said. You lost money on it the year before too.

I've been losing money on that vineyard ever since I bought it, my uncle said. Who wants grapes? Who wants raisins?

It may be different this year, I said.

Do you think so? my uncle said.

I think this Mexican is going to do the trick, I said.

That's funny, my uncle said. I've been thinking the same

thing. If he feeds them thirteen mouths this winter, not counting his own, it won't be so bad this year.

You can't lose more than you lost last year, I said.

The Japs are all right, my uncle said, only they don't look at things the way Mexicans do.

The Japs wouldn't think of keeping four ordinary dogs, I said.

They'd drive the dogs away, my uncle said.

They'd throw rocks at the dogs, I said.

I think I'm going to have a good year this year, my uncle said.

We didn't say anything more all the way into town.

The Messenger

Clarence Acough was ten years old and on his way home from school, in 1918, when Jeff Willis called him into the drug store on Mariposa Street and said, Son, Judge Olson's mother is dying and I want you to run over to Doc Gregory's house on Blackstone Avenue and tell him to come right down for the medicine and then hurry out to Malaga to Judge Olson's house. Doc Gregory'll probably be drunk, but splash some cold water on his face and if he sicks the dog on you, call the dog by its name, Hamilton, and it won't bite you. Otherwise it will. Splash six or seven cups of cold water on Doc's face and get him into the Ford and come back to the store with him. I'd go myself, but I got to stay in the store and take care of the soda fountain trade.

The little boy was pretty confused. In the first place, he hadn't ever talked to Jeff Willis before, although he had seen him in the window of the drug store many times, changing the attractions around, especially the mechanical dummy boy that licked an ice-cream cone and shook its head from side to side, delighted with the taste of ice-cream. Otherwise Clarence didn't know Jeff, and Jeff didn't know Clarence, and the little boy was confused and excited about the whole thing, especially the dog.

Hamilton.

He would have run right out of the store and done his duty, but he didn't like the part about Hamilton the dog, although he was somewhat anxious about Judge Olson's mother in Malaga. It was exciting all right, but it was just a little too exciting. So many names of people and places were involved that Clarence didn't know who or where, so he made for the door, then turned around, almost moving in two directions, wanting to get the good deed done, wanting to do it right, remembering the dog Hamilton, and said, *What?*

Judge Olson's old lady, Jeff Willis said, She's dying, son. She's had another stroke and it looks like she ain't going to pull through and see another County Fair. Out in Malaga. She's a hundred and two. The Judge is over seventy himself, and he's all upset, and the only man in the world who can keep her alive until the Judge takes her to another County Fair is Doc Gregory, and you got to run right out to his house on Blackstone Avenue and splash cold water on his face. You can't miss it. It's the house with the two cement lions on the front lawn.

On his way home from school, Clarence had been dreaming about adventure, and he had been feeling melancholy about the dullness of everything, and he had been kicking pebbles along the sidewalk and street, dreaming of adventure and being melancholy about being a small boy and having to go to school every day and never being able to really enjoy living. He had kicked one pebble two blocks out of his way, and that's how he had gotten on Mariposa Street.

Yes, sir, he said to Jeff. The house with the two cement lions on the front lawn.

Is it a big dog?

It's the biggest kind of dog there is, the druggist said. A St. Bernard, but if you call it by its name, Hamilton, it won't bite you.

Yes, sir, the boy said. Hamilton. Splash water on his face and tell him Judge Olson's mother is dying.

Now you got it, the druggist said. Run right out there. It's only six blocks. You'll be there in no time. What's your name?

Clarence, the boy said.

All right, Clarence, the druggist said. Here's a package of chewing gum for you.

I don't want anything, the boy said, I'll run right out there.

He ran out of the store, looking back six or seven times in two seconds, and ran into the middle of a large lady who immediately exhaled a mournful groan. He begged the lady's pardon and began running up the street full speed.

While the boy was running up the street, Jeff tried to comfort the lady.

Judge Olson's old lady, Jeff said. She's dying. I sent the boy to Doc Gregory's house. Doc'll probably be drunk, but I told the boy what to do.

I'd go for the doctor myself, Jeff said, only I got to take care of the soda fountain trade.

Well, Jeff Willis never served more than three drinks a day over the soda fountain and there was no trade. Not more than seven people ever passed his store in an hour. He just thought he was running a business, and he didn't want to change his opinion at the last minute after ten years of sustained effort.

The lady asked for a glass of water, please. Jeff raced around behind the counter and got a glass and filled it with luke-warm water and placed it neatly on the tiled counter.

Clarence Acough got very tired after running a block, but he couldn't so much as think of slowing down. At the end of the second block, though, he couldn't keep it up, so he sat on the curb to rest. It was very warm and he was sticky with sweat, and all of a sudden everything that had always seemed common and dull to his eye now seemed exciting and wonderful. Out in Malaga the poor old lady was dying and most likely she wouldn't live to see the next County Fair. She would be *dead.* She wouldn't be able to see *anything.* Consciously, he studied the fine white house across the street, with the two enormous eucalyptus trees, and the telephone poles, and the street, and everything else visible.

It was good to be alive.

He was breathing hard, feeling how swell it was to be able to look around and see things, when Doris Barnes and Grover Stone came across the street and stood before him. Well, Doris Barnes was the one magical person in the world to Clarence Acough, and Grover Stone was the one boy in the world Clarence couldn't tolerate. When Clarence saw the boy and girl together he began again, in less than a fraction of a second, to feel melancholy about the way things were, especially Doris walking home with Grover. The trouble with Grover, primarily, was that he always wore good shoes and always had five or ten cents in his pocket. Consequently, he imagined he was something.

The little girl said, What's the matter?

If Clarence hadn't been sore about the way Grover was standing over him and looking down, he would have explained about Judge Olson's mother dying in Malaga, Doc Gregory, Jeff Willis, the County Fair, and the dog Hamilton. Clarence would have jumped up and gone on down the street, toward the doctor's house, with the two cement lions on the lawn. He would have done his duty, but he began to forget about the old lady in Malaga and he began to feel bitter about Doris walking home with a guy like Grover.

It was very warm. He was sticky, and nothing ever happened.

Nothing's the matter, Clarence said. I guess I can sit down and rest if I feel like it.

Clarence figured maybe Doris would have sense enough to know from the way he talked how much he loved her, but he was wrong. Doris didn't like the way he talked, and neither did Grover. Grover thought he would have some fun, being smart, and he said, Clarence Acough thinks he's tough.

Clarence jumped up and said, You think you're smart.

In the drug store on Mariposa Street Jeff Willis was walking around in a circle when the telephone rang. It was Judge Olson, in Malaga. He wanted to know where in hell Doc Gregory was.

I just sent a boy to get him, Jeff said. Doc'll be out to your place in no time. How's your mother?

I don't know for sure, Judge Olson said. She seems to be dead, but I guess she's sleeping.

Is she breathing? Jeff Willis said.

I don't know for sure, Judge Olson said. I don't think so.

Are you sure? Jeff Willis said.

She doesn't seem to be breathing, Judge Olson said. Where in hell is Doc Gregory?

I sent a boy named Clarence to get him, Jeff said. I told him what to do about the dog.

Grover Stone said, I *am* smart.

And he made a very smart face.

Clarence couldn't help it: he hit Grover on the left ear, and Grover hit him on the nose. Clarence felt the pain very sharply and began chasing Grover toward town, away from the house with the two cement lions on the front lawn. Clarence chased Grover four blocks, but Grover got away. Clarence was too tired to go on chasing him.

Doris Barnes hadn't kept up with them. She was probably home, sitting on the front porch.

She herself.

Clarence began walking toward her house and when he reached the house, she *wasn't* sitting on the front porch. He sat on the curb across the street and waited for her to come out of the house. She was the loveliest creature in the world. And she was in the house. She was somewhere in the house, and maybe she would come out, and he would see her. He would see the net white dress she wore, and he would see her clean round face with the amazing eyes and nose and lips and the amazing brown hair. Doris Barnes. Maybe she would come out of the house and go to the store for a can of peaches or something. Maybe she would talk to him. Maybe she would *like* him.

When it began to be dark, he decided maybe she wouldn't come out of the house. Then he decided maybe she *would.*

She didn't, though, so he got up, feeling very tired, and confused, and began walking home. He was almost home when he began to remember that he had forgotten something. He began to walk very slowly and little by little it came back to him: the old lady out in Malaga, dying. Doc Gregory in the house with the two cement lions on the front lawn, drunk, and the dog Hamilton.

He was very hungry, very tired, and very sleepy, and Doc Gregory's house on Blackstone Avenue seemed very far away. He guessed he ought to turn around and run like anything all the way to Doc Gregory's house and splash six or seven glasses of water on his face and call the dog Hamilton and get Doc into the Ford and rush down to Jeff Willis's drug store and get the medicine and drive forty miles an hour down the highway to Judge Olson's house in Malaga and give the old lady the medicine and keep her alive long enough to see the next County Fair, but maybe she was already dead, or maybe Doc Gregory wasn't home, maybe he was somewhere in town, drinking, or if the old lady wasn't dead, maybe she'd be dead by the time Doc Gregory got out to the house in Malaga with the medicine, if he was home, and Clarence was so tired he didn't think it would make much difference if Doc Gregory *did* keep her alive a year or two more, she would be sure to die after a year or two anyway, so he didn't turn around and run back to the house on Blackstone Avenue.

She'd probably die in a year or two anyway.

He staggered home and ate supper and right after supper he fell asleep, and in the morning he forgot all about it, remembering Doris Barnes, and he kept on forgetting all about it, and three months later father moved the family a hundred miles up the highway to Modesto, and Clarence Acough kept on forgetting the old lady in Malaga, and after a while he even forgot Doris Barnes, and then one day in August, in 1926, eight years later, when he was eighteen years old, he remembered Doris, and three seconds later he remembered the old lady in Malaga, dying, and he was driving a second-hand Studebaker home from Junior College, and he drove right past his house, and on down the highway, and three hours later just before it got to be dark he reached the old home town and drove down Mariposa Street, looking for Jeff Willis's drug store, and found it.

He went in and Jeff was standing behind the counter, taking care of the soda fountain trade. Jeff was delighted to see a young man parking a car in front of his store and coming in and sitting on a stool at the counter.

What'll it be? Jeff said.

What I want to know, Clarence Acough said, is: *Did she get to see the County Fair?*

Who? Jeff said.

You don't remember me, Clarence said. I'm sorry I didn't get out to Doc Gregory's house on Blackstone Avenue, but something happened on the way.

What? said Jeff.

Don't you remember? Clarence said. You told me to run out to Doc Gregory's house on Blackstone Avenue. The house with the two cement lions on the front lawn. And throw six or seven glasses of cold water on his face if he was drunk. And to be careful about the dog Hamilton. Remember?

Jeff thought about it carefully, making a face.

Oh, yes, he said, I remember. That was *ten, fifteen* years ago.

No, Clarence said, eight years ago.

Judge Olson's mother, Jeff said. I remember. Sure.

I'm sorry I never did get out to Doc Gregory's house, Clarence said. I feel pretty bad about that. Did she ever get to see the County Fair? Did Doc Gregory come down in his Ford and pick up the medicine and drive out to the house in Malaga and save her life? How did it turn out?

She was stone dead before you left this store, Jeff Willis said. Coroner Fielding claimed she had been dead three days. They took Judge Olson up to Napa to the asylum. They claimed he was crazy from old age, but he wasn't much over seventy. He's still up there for all I know.

I don't suppose the medicine would have done her any good, Clarence said.

Well, I don't know, Jeff Willis said. Coroner Fielding claimed she had been dead three days, but Judge Olson claimed she wasn't dead at all. He claimed she was sleeping. Coroner Fielding was the kind of man to exaggerate a good deal, and I don't know for sure if a little medicine wouldn't have straightened everything out.

What about Doc Gregory? Clarence said. I never did get to see Doc Gregory.

Well, nobody's seen much of Doc Gregory lately, Jeff said. He don't go out much. He just stays home and drinks.

How about the dog? Clarence said. Hamilton.

Hamilton died about three years ago, Jeff said.

The young man looked up at the signs over the mirror and read the descriptions of the magnificent things Jeff Willis prepared for the soda fountain trade. He felt pretty sad about everything, a mournful nostalgia for something impossible to define, great loneliness, partly because it was nightfall, partly because he didn't know whatever became of Doris Barnes, partly because the old lady had been dead three days anyway, partly because Judge Olson was in the asylum, partly because Doc Gregory didn't go out any more: nevertheless, he said, I'd like a special de luxe chocolate sundae with walnuts, and Jeff, after waiting eighteen years, started jumping around with glass dishes, ice-cream scoops, and fancy spoons.

Many Miles Per Hour

We used to see him going down the highway fifty miles an hour, and my brother Mike used to look kind of sore and jealous.

There he goes, Mike used to say. Where in hell do you think he's going?

Nowhere, I guess, I used to say.

He's in a pretty big hurry for a man who's going nowhere.

I guess he's just turning her loose to see how fast she'll go.

She goes fast enough, Mike used to say. Where the hell can he go from here? Fowler, that's where. That good-for-nothing town.

Or Hanford, I used to say. Or Bakersfield. Don't forget Bakersfield, because it's on the highway. He could make it in three hours.

Two, Mike used to say. He could make it in an hour and three quarters.

Mike was twelve and I was ten, and in those days, 1918, a coupé was a funny-looking affair, an apple-box on four wheels. It wasn't easy to get any kind of a car to go fifty miles an hour, let alone a Ford coupé, but we figured this man had fixed up the motor of his car. We figured he had made a racer out of his little yellow coupé.

We used to see the automobile every day, going down the highway toward Fowler, and an hour or so later we used to see it coming back. On the way down, the car would be traveling like a bat out of hell, rattling and shaking and bouncing, and the man in the car would be smoking a cigarette and smiling to himself, like somebody a little crazy. But on the way back, it would be going no more than ten miles an hour, and the man at the wheel would be calm and sort of slumped down, kind of tired.

He was a fellow you couldn't tell anything about. You couldn't tell how old he was, or what nationality, or anything else. He certainly wasn't more than forty, although he might be less than thirty; and he certainly wasn't Italian, Greek, Armenian, Russian, Chinese, Japanese, German, or any of the other nationalities we knew.

I figure he's an American, Mike used to say. I figure he's a salesman of some kind. He hurries down the highway to some little town and sells something, and comes back, taking it easy.

Maybe, I used to say.

But I didn't think so. I figured he was more likely to be a guy who *liked* to drive down the highway in a big hurry, just for the devil of it.

Those were the years of automobile races: Dario Resta, Jimmie Murphy, Jimmie Chevrolet, and a lot of other boys who finally got killed in racetrack accidents. Those were the days when everybody in America was getting acquainted with the idea of speed. My brother Mike often thought of getting some money somewhere and buying a second-hand car and fixing it up and making it go very fast. Sixty miles an hour maybe. He thought that would be something to do. It was the money, though, that he didn't have.

When I buy my hack, Mike used to say, you're going to see some real speed.

You ain't going to buy no hack, I used to say. What you going to buy a hack with?

I'll get money some way, Mike used to say.

The highway passed in front of our house on Railroad Avenue, just a half-mile south of Rosenberg's Dried Fruit Packing House. Rosenberg's was four brothers who bought figs, dried peaches, apricots, nectarines, and raisins, and put them up in nice cartons and sent them all over the country, and even to foreign countries in Europe. Every summer they hired a lot of people from our part of town, and the women packed the stuff, and the men did harder work, with hand-trucks. Mike went down for a job, but one of the brothers told him to wait another year till he got a little huskier.

That was better than nothing, and Mike couldn't wait to get huskier. He used to look at the pulp-paper magazines for the advertisements of guys like Lionel Strongfort and Earl Liederman, them giants of physical culture, them big guys who could lift a sack of flour over their heads with one arm, and a lot of other things. Mike used to wonder how them big guys got that way, and he used to go down to Cosmos Playground and practice chinning himself on the crossbars, and he used to do a lot of running to develop the muscles of his legs. Mike got to be pretty solid, but not much huskier than he had been. When the hot weather came Mike stopped training. It was too hot to bother.

We started sitting on the steps of our front porch, watching the cars go by. In front of the highway were the railroad tracks, and we could look north and south for miles because it was all level land. We could see a locomotive coming south from town, and we could sit on the steps of our front porch and watch it come closer and closer, and hear it too, and then we could look north and watch it disappear. We did that all one summer during school vacation.

There goes locomotive S. P. 797, Mike used to say.

Yes, sir.

There goes Santa Fe 485321, I used to say. What do you figure is in that box-car, Mike?

Raisins, Mike used to say. Rosenberg's raisins, or figs, or dried peaches, or apricots. Boy, I'll be glad when next summer rolls around, so I can go to work at Rosenberg's and buy me that hack.

Boy, I used to say.

Just thinking of working at Rosenberg's used to do something to Mike. He used to jump up and start shadow-boxing, puffing like a professional fighter, pulling up his tights every once in a while, and grunting.

Boy.

Boy, what he was going to do at Rosenberg's.

It was hell for Mike not to have a job at Rosenberg's, making money, so he could buy his old hack and fix the motor and make it go sixty miles an hour. He used to talk about the old hack all day, sitting on the steps of the porch and watching the cars and trains go by. When the yellow Ford coupé showed up, Mike used to get a little sore, because it was fast. It made him jealous to think of that fellow in the fast car, going down the highway fifty miles an hour.

When I get my hack, Mike used to say, I'll show that guy what real speed is.

We used to walk to town every once in a while. Actually it was at least once every day, but the days were so long every day seemed like a week and it would seem like we hadn't been to town for a week, although we had been there the day before. We used to walk to town, and around town, and then back home again. There was nowhere to go and nothing to do, but we used to get a kick out of walking by the garages and used-car lots on Broadway, especially Mike.

One day we saw the yellow Ford coupé in Ben Mallock's garage on Broadway, and Mike grabbed me by the arm.

There it is, Joe, he said. There's that racer. Let's go in.

We went in and stood by the car. There was no one around, and it was very quiet.

Then the man who owned the car stuck his head out from underneath the car. He looked like the happiest man in the world.

Hello, Mike said.

Howdy, boys, said the man who owned the yellow coupé.

Something wrong? said Mike.

Nothing serious, said the man. Just keeping the old boat in shape.

You don't know us, said Mike. We live in that white house on Railroad Avenue, near Walnut. We see you going down the highway every day.

Oh, yes, said the man. I thought I'd seen you boys somewhere.

My brother Mike, I said, says you're a salesman.

He's wrong, said the man.

I waited for him to tell us *what* he was, if he wasn't a salesman, but he didn't say anything.

I'm going to buy a car myself next year, said Mike. I figure I'll get me a fast Chevrolet.

He did a little shadow-boxing, just thinking about the car, and then he got self-conscious, and the man busted out laughing.

Great idea, he said. Great idea.

He crawled out from under the car and lit a cigarette.

I figure you go about fifty miles an hour, said Mike.

Fifty-two to be exact, said the man. I hope to make sixty one of these days.

I could see Mike liked the fellow very much, and I knew I liked him. He was younger than we had imagined. He was probably no more than twenty-five, but he acted no older than a boy of fifteen or sixteen. We thought he was great.

Mike said, What's your name?

Mike could ask a question like that without sounding silly.

Bill, said the man. Bill Wallace. Everybody calls me Speed Wallace.

My name's Mike Flor, said Mike. I'm pleased to meet you. This is my brother Joe.

Mike and the man shook hands. Mike began to shadow-box again.

How would you boys like a little ride? Speed Wallace said.

Oh boy, said Mike.

We jumped into the yellow coupé, and Speed drove out of the garage, down Broadway, and across the railroad tracks in front of Rosenberg's where the highway began. On the highway he opened up to show us a little speed. We passed our house in no time and pretty soon we were tearing down the highway forty miles an hour, then forty-five, then fifty, and pretty soon the speedometer said fifty-one, fifty-two, fifty-three, and the car was rattling like anything.

By the time we were going fifty-six miles an hour we were in Fowler and the man slowed the car down, then stopped. It was very hot.

How about a cold drink? he said.

We got out of the car and walked into a store. Mike drank a bottle of strawberry, and so did I, and then the man said to have another. I said no, but Mike drank another.

The man drank four bottles of strawberry.

Then we got into the car and he drove back very slowly, not more than ten miles an hour, talking all the time about the car, and how fine it was to be able to go down a highway fifty miles an hour.

Do you make money? Mike said.

Not a nickel, Speed said. But one of these days I'm going to build myself a racer and get into the County Fair races, and make some money.

Boy, said Mike.

He let us off at our house, and we talked about the ride for three hours straight.

It was swell. Speed Wallace was a great guy.

In September the County Fair opened. There was a dirt track out there, a mile around. We read advertising cards on fences that said there would be automobile races out there this year.

One day we noticed that the yellow Ford coupé hadn't gone down the highway a whole week.

Mike jumped up all of a sudden when he realized it.

That guy's in the races at the Fair, he said. Come on, let's go.

And we started running down Railroad Avenue.

It was nine in the morning and the races wouldn't begin till around two-thirty, but we ran just the same.

We had to get to the Fair grounds early so we could sneak in. It took us an hour and a half to walk and run to the Fair Grounds, and then it took us two hours more to sneak in. We were caught twice, but finally we got in.

We climbed into the grandstand and everything looked okey-dokey. There were two racing cars on the track, one black, and the other green.

After a while the black one started going around the track. When it got around to where we were sitting we both jumped up because the guy at the wheel was the man who owned the yellow coupé. We felt swell. Boy, he went fast and made a lot of noise. And plenty of dust too, going around the corners.

The races didn't start at two-thirty, they started at three. The grandstands were full of excited people. Seven racing cars got in line. Each was cranked, and the noise they made was very loud and very exciting. Then the race started and Mike started acting like a crazy man, talking to himself, shadow-boxing, and jumping around.

It was the first race, a short one, twenty miles, and Speed Wallace came in fourth.

The next race was forty miles, and Speed Wallace came in second.

The third and last race was seventy-five miles, seventy-five times around the track, and the thirtieth time around Speed Wallace got out in front, just a little way, but out in front just the same: then something went wrong, the inside front wheel of Speed Wallace's racing car busted off and the car turned a furious somersault, away up into the air. Everybody saw Speed Wallace fly out of the car. Everybody saw the car smash him against the wooden fence.

Mike started running down the grandstand, to get closer. I ran after him and I could hear him swearing.

The race didn't stop, but a lot of mechanics got Speed Wallace's wrecked car out of the way, and carried Speed Wallace to an ambulance. While the other cars were going around the track for the seventieth time a man got up and told the people Speed Wallace had been instantly killed.

Holy Christ.

That fellow, Mike said, he got killed. That fellow who used to go down the highway in that yellow Ford coupé, he got killed, Joe. That fellow who gave us a ride to Fowler and bought us drinks.

When it got dark, walking home, Mike started to cry. Just a little. I could tell he was crying from the way his voice sounded. He wasn't really crying.

You remember that swell guy, Joe, he said. He was the one who got killed.

We started sitting on the steps of our front porch again, watching the cars go by, but it was sad. We knew the fellow in the yellow Ford coupé wouldn't go down the highway again. Every once in a while Mike would jump up and start shadow-boxing, only it wasn't the way it used to be. He wasn't happy any more, he was sore, and it looked like he was trying to knock hell out of something in the world that caused such a lousy thing like that to happen to a guy like Speed Wallace.

Sweetheart Sweetheart Sweetheart

One thing she *could* do was play the piano and sing. She couldn't cook or anything like that. Anyhow she didn't like to cook because she couldn't make pastry anyway and that's what she liked. She was something like the pastry she was always eating, big and soft and pink, and like a child although she was probably in her late thirties. She claimed she'd been on the stage. *I was an actress three seasons,* is what she told the boy's mother. His mother liked the neighbor but couldn't exactly figure her out. She was married and had no kids, that's what his mother couldn't figure out; and she spent all her time making dresses and putting them on and being very pretty.

Who for? his mother would ask his sister. She would be busy in the kitchen getting food cooked or making bread and in English, which she couldn't talk well but which she liked to talk when she was talking about the neighbor, she said. What for, she's so anxious to be pretty? And then in Italian she'd say, But my, how nice she plays the piano. She's a good neighbor to have.

They'd just moved from one side of town to the other, from Italian town to where the Americans were. This lady was one of them, an American, so his mother guessed that was the way they were, like fancy things to eat, sweet and creamy and soft and pink.

The neighbor used to come over a lot because, she said, it was so refreshing to be among real people.

You know, Mrs. Amendola, she used to say, it's a pleasure to have a neighbor like you. It's so wonderful the way you take care of all your wonderful children without a husband. All your fine growing girls and boys.

Oh, his mother used to laugh, the kids are good. I feed them and take care of them. Headache, toothache, trouble at school, I take care of everything; and his mother roared with laughter. Then his mother looked at the neighbor and said, They're my kids. We fight, we yell, we hit each other, but we like each other. You no got children?

No, the neighbor said. The boy became embarrassed. His mother was so boisterous and abrupt and direct. It was about the third time she'd asked if the neighbor had no children. What she meant, he knew, was, How come you haven't got any? A big woman like you, full of everything to make children?

The neighbor used to come over often when her husband was away. He covered the valley from Bakersfield to Sacramento, selling hardware. Sometimes his wife went with him, but most often not.

She preferred not to because travel was so difficult. And yet whenever she didn't go that meant that she would be in the house alone, and that made her lonely, so she used to visit the Italian family.

One night she came over sobbing and his mother put her arms around the neighbor as if she was one of his mother's kids, and comforted her.

But one thing he noticed that kind of puzzled him; she

wasn't *really* crying. It wasn't honest-to-God crying; it was something else; she wasn't hurt or sorry or in pain or anything; it seemed like she just felt like crying, so she cried, just the same as if she might have felt like buying a dozen cream puffs and eating them. That's the impression he got.

Oh, Mrs. Amendola, she said. I was sitting all alone in the house when all of a sudden I began to remember all the years and then I got scared and started to cry. Oh, I feel so bad, she said and then smiled in a way that seemed awfully lovely to the boy and awfully strange. She looked around at his sister, and then, smiling, she looked at him and he didn't know what to do. She looked a long time. It wasn't a glance. And he knew right away something he didn't understand was going on. She was awfully lovely, big and soft and full of everything, and he felt embarrassed. Her arms were so full.

The little kids were all in bed, so it was only his mother and his sister and him. His mother said, You be all right. You sit with us and talk, you be fine. What's the matter?

I feel so sad, the neighbor said. When I remember all the years gone by, the times when I was a little girl, and then when I was almost grown-up at high school, and then on the stage, I feel so lonely.

Oh, you be all right, his mother said. You like a glass of wine?

His mother didn't wait for her to answer. She got out the bottle and poured two drinks, one for herself and one for the neighbor.

Drink wine, his mother said. Wine is good.

The neighbor sipped the wine.

Oh, it's wonderful, she said. You're a wonderful family, Mrs. Amendola. Won't you come to my house for a visit? I'd like to show you the house.

Oh, sure, his mother said. His mother wanted to see what

her house looked like. So they all went to the house next door and room by room the neighbor showed them the house. It was just like her, like cream puffs. Soft and warm and pink, all except *his* room. He had his own room, bed and everything. There was something fishy somewhere, the boy thought. Americans were different from Italians, that's all he knew. If he slept in one bed and she in another, something was funny somewhere. Her room was like a place in another world. It was so like a woman that he felt ashamed to go in. He stood in the doorway while his mother and sister admired the beautiful room, and then the neighbor noticed him and took his hand. He felt excited and wished he was with her that way alone and in another world. The neighbor laughed and said, But I want *you* to admire my room, too, Tommy. You're such an intelligent and refined boy.

He didn't know for sure, maybe it was his imagination, but when she said he was intelligent and refined it seemed to him she squeezed his hand. He was awfully scared, almost sick. He didn't know about the Americans yet, and he didn't want to do anything wrong. Maybe she *had* squeezed his hand, but maybe it was as if she was just an older person, or a relative. Maybe it was because she was their neighbor, nothing else. He took his hand away as quickly as possible. He didn't speak about the room because he knew anything he'd say would be ridiculous. It was a place he'd like to get in and stay in forever, with her. And that was crazy. She was married. She was old enough to be his mother, although she was a lot younger than his mother. But that was what he wanted.

After they saw the house she cooked chocolate and brought them a cup each. The cups were very delicate and beautiful. There was a plate full of mixed pastry, all kinds of it. She made each of them eat a lot; anyway, for every one she ate, she made them eat one, too, so they each ate four, then there were two left. She laughed and said she could never get enough of pastry, so she was going to take one of the last two, and since Tommy was the man present, he ought to take the other. She said that in a way that more than ever excited the boy. He became confused and deeply mournful about the whole thing. It was something new and out of the world. It was like wanting to get out of the world and never come back. To get into the strange region of warmth and beauty and ease and something else that she seemed to make him feel existed, by her voice and her way of laughing and the way she was, the way her house was, especially the way she looked at him.

He wondered if his mother and sister knew about it. He hoped they didn't. After the chocolate and pastry, his mother asked her to play the piano and sing and she was only too glad to. She played three songs; one for his mother; one for his sister; and then she said, This one for Tommy. She played and sang, *Maytime,* the song that hollers or screams, *Sweetheart sweetheart sweetheart.* The boy was very flattered. He hoped his mother and sister didn't catch on, but that was silly because the first thing his mother said when they got home was, Tommy, I think you got a sweetheart now. And his mother roared with laughter.

She's crazy about you, his sister said.

His sister was three years older than him, seventeen, and she had a fellow. She didn't know yet if she was going to marry him.

She's just nice, the boy said. She was nice to all of us. That's the way she is.

Oh, no, his sister said. She was *nicer* to you than to us. She's falling in love with you, Tommy. Are you falling in love with her?

Aw, shut up, the boy said.

You see, Ma, his sister said. He *is* falling in love with her.

Tell her to cut it out, Ma, the boy said.

You leave my boy alone, his mother told his sister.

And then his mother roared with laughter. It was such a wonderful joke. His mother and his sister laughed until he had to laugh, too. Then all of a sudden their laughter became louder and heartier than ever. It was *too* loud.

Let's not laugh so loud, the boy said. Suppose she hears us? She'll think we're laughing at *her.*

He's in love, Ma, his sister said.

His mother shrugged her shoulders. He knew she was going to come out with one of her comic remarks and he hoped it wouldn't be too embarrassing.

She's a nice girl, his mother said, and his sister started laughing again.

He decided not to think about her any more. He knew if he did his mother and sister would know about it and make fun of him. It wasn't a thing you could make fun of. It was a thing like nothing else, most likely the best thing of all. He didn't want it to be made fun of. He couldn't explain to them but he felt they shouldn't laugh about it.

In the morning her piano-playing wakened him and he began to feel the way he'd felt last night when she'd taken his hand, only now it was worse. He didn't want to get up, or anything. What he wished was that they were together in a room like hers, out of the world, away from everybody, for ever. She sang the song again, four choruses of it, *Sweetheart sweetheart sweetheart.*

His mother made him get up. What's the matter? she said. You'll be late for work. Are you sick?

No, he said. What time is it?

He jumped out of bed and got into his clothes and ate and got on his wheel and raced to the grocery store. He was only two minutes late.

The romance kept up the whole month, all of August. Her

husband came home for two days about the middle of the month. He fooled around in the yard and then went away again.

The boy didn't know what would ever happen. She came over two or three times every week. She appeared in the yard when he was in the yard. She invited the family over to her house two or three times for chocolate and pastry. She woke him up almost every morning singing *Sweetheart sweetheart sweetheart.*

His mother and sister still kidded him about her every once in a while.

One night in September when he got home his sister and mother had a big laugh about him and the neighbor.

Too bad, his mother said. Here, eat your supper. Too bad.

We feel sorry for you, his sister said.

What are you talking about? the boy said.

It's too late now, his mother said.

Too late for *what?* the boy said.

You waited too long, his sister said.

Aw, cut it out, the boy said. What are you talking about?

She's got another sweetheart now, his sister said.

He felt stunned, disgusted, and ill, but tried to go on eating and tried not to show how he felt.

Who? he said.

Your sweetheart, his sister said. You know *who.*

He wasn't sorry. He was angry. Not at his sister and mother; at *her*. She was stupid. He tried to laugh it off.

Well, it's about time, he said.

He comes and gets her in his car, his sister said. It's a Cadillac.

What about her husband? the boy said. He felt foolish.

He don't know! his mother said. Maybe he don't *care*. He's dead, I think.

His mother roared with laughter, and then his sister, too,

and then he, too. He was glad Italians laughed, anyway. That made him feel a little better. After supper, though, he was strangely ill all the time. She was a stupid, foolish woman.

Every night for a week his mother and sister told him about the man coming and getting her every afternoon, driving off with her in his Cadillac.

She's got no family, his mother said. She's right. What's the use being pretty for nothing?

He's an awful handsome man, his sister said.

The husband, his mother said, he's dead.

They told him about the neighbor and her lover every night for a week, and then one night she came over to pay another visit. She was lovelier than ever, and not sad any more. Not even make-believe sad.

He was afraid his mother would ask about the man, so he tried to keep her from doing so. He kept looking into his mother's eyes and telling her not to make any mistakes. It would be all right across the tracks, but not in this neighborhood. If *she* wanted to come out with it herself, *she* could tell them. She didn't, though. The boy waited five minutes and then decided she wasn't going to say anything.

He got his cap and said, I'm going to the library, Ma.

All right, his mother said.

He didn't say good night to her. He didn't even look at her. She knew *why,* too.

After that she never played the piano in the mornings, and whenever she *did* play the piano she didn't play the song she'd said was for him.

The Great Leapfrog Contest

Rosie Mahoney was a tough little Irish kid whose folks, through some miscalculation in directions, or out of an innate spirit of anarchy, had moved into the Russian-Italian-and-Greek neighborhood of my home town, across the Southern Pacific tracks, around G Street.

She wore a turtleneck sweater, usually red. Her father was a bricklayer named Cull and a heavy drinker. Her mother's name was Mary. Mary Mahoney used to go to the Greek Orthodox Catholic Church on Kearny Boulevard every Sunday, because there was no Irish Church to go to anywhere in the neighborhood. The family seemed to be a happy one.

Rosie's three brothers had all grown up and gone to sea. Her two sisters had married. Rosie was the last of the clan. She had entered the world when her father had been close to sixty and her mother in her early fifties. For all that, she was hardly the studious or scholarly type.

Rosie had little use for girls, and as far as possible avoided them. She had less use for boys, but found it undesirable to avoid them. That is to say, she made it a point to take part in everything the boys did. She was always on hand, and always the first to take up any daring or crazy idea. Everybody felt awkward about her continuous presence, but it was no use trying to chase her away, because that meant a fight in which she asked no quarter, and gave none.

If she didn't whip every boy she fought, every fight was at least an honest draw, with a slight edge in Rosie's favor. She didn't fight girl-style, or cry if hurt. She fought the regular style and took advantage of every opening. It was very humiliating to be hurt by Rosie, so after a while any boy who thought of trying to chase her away, decided not to.

It was no use. She just wouldn't go. She didn't seem to like any of the boys especially, but she liked being in on any mischief they might have in mind, and she wanted to play on any teams they organized. She was an excellent baseball player, being as good as anybody else in the neighborhood at any position, and for her age an expert pitcher. She had a wicked wing, too, and could throw a ball in from left field so that when it hit the catcher's mitt it made a nice sound.

She was extraordinarily swift on her feet and played a beautiful game of tin-can hockey.

At pee-wee, she seemed to have the most disgusting luck in the world.

At the game we invented and used to call *Horse* she was as good at *horse* as at *rider,* and she insisted on following the rules of the game. She insisted on being horse when it was her turn to be horse. This always embarrassed her partner, whoever he happened to be, because it didn't seem right for a boy to be getting up on the back of a girl.

She was an excellent football player too.

As a matter of fact, she was just naturally the equal of any boy in the neighborhood, and much the superior of many of them. Especially after she had lived in the neighborhood three years. It took her that long to make everybody understand that she had come to stay and that she was *going* to stay.

She did, too; even after the arrival of a boy named Rex Folger, who was from somewhere in the south of Texas. This boy Rex was a natural-born leader. Two months after his arrival in the neighborhood, it was understood by everyone that if Rex wasn't the leader of the gang, he was very nearly the leader. He had fought and licked every boy in the neighborhood who at one time or another had fancied himself leader. And he had done so without any noticeable ill-feeling, pride, or ambition.

As a matter of fact, no one could possibly have been more good-natured than Rex. Everybody resented him, just the same.

One winter, the whole neighborhood took to playing a game that had become popular on the other side of the tracks, in another slum neighborhood of the town: *Leapfrog*. The idea was for as many boys as cared to participate, to bend down and be leaped over by every other boy in the game, and then himself to get up and begin leaping over all the other boys, and then bend down again until all the boys had leaped over him again, and keep this up until all the other players had become exhausted. This didn't happen, sometimes, until the last two players had traveled a distance of three or four miles, while the other players walked along, watching and making bets.

Rosie, of course, was always in on the game. She was always one of the last to drop out, too. And she was the only person in the neighborhood Rex Folger hadn't fought and beaten.

He felt that that was much too humiliating even to think about. But inasmuch as she seemed to be a member of the gang, he felt that in some way or another he ought to prove his superiority.

One summer day during vacation, an argument between Rex and Rosie developed and Rosie pulled off her turtleneck sweater and challenged him to a fight. Rex took a cigarette from his pocket, lighted it, inhaled, and told Rosie he wasn't in the habit of hitting women—where he came from that amounted to boxing your mother. On the other hand, he said, if Rosie cared to compete with him in any other sport, he would be glad to oblige her. Rex was a very calm and courteous conversationalist. He had poise. It was unconscious, of course, but he had it just the same. He was just naturally a man who couldn't be hurried, flustered, or excited.

So Rex and Rosie fought it out in this game Leapfrog. They got to leaping over one another, quickly, too, until the first thing we knew the whole gang of us was out on the State Highway going south towards Fowler. It was a very hot day. Rosie and Rex were in great shape, and it looked like one was tougher than the other and more stubborn. They talked a good deal, especially Rosie, who insisted that she would have to fall down unconscious before she'd give up to a guy like Rex.

He said he was sorry his opponent was a girl. It grieved him deeply to have to make a girl exert herself to the point of death, but it was just too bad. He had to, so he had to. They leaped and squatted, leaped and squatted, and we got out to Sam Day's vineyard. That was half-way to Fowler. It didn't seem like either Rosie or Rex were ever going to get tired. They hadn't even begun to show signs of growing tired, although each of them was sweating a great deal.

Naturally, we were sure Rex would win the contest. But that was because we hadn't taken into account the fact that he was a simple person, whereas Rosie was crafty and shrewd. Rosie knew how to figure angles. She had discovered how to jump over Rex Folger in a way that weakened him. And after a while, about three miles out of Fowler, we noticed that she was coming down on Rex's *neck,* instead of on his back. Naturally, this was hurting him and making the blood rush to his head. Rosie herself squatted in such a way that it was impossible, almost, for Rex to get anywhere near her neck with his hands.

Before long, we noticed that Rex was weakening. His head was getting closer and closer to the ground. About a half mile out of Fowler, we heard Rex's head bumping the ground every time Rosie leaped over him. They were good loud bumps that we knew were painful, but Rex wasn't complaining. He was too proud to complain.

Rosie, on the other hand, knew she had her man, and she was giving him all she had. She was bumping his head on the ground as solidly as she could, because she knew she didn't have much more fight in her, and if she didn't lay him out cold, in the hot sun, in the next ten minutes or so, she would fall down exhausted herself, and lose the contest.

Suddenly Rosie bumped Rex's head a real powerful one. He got up very dazed and very angry. It was the first time we had ever seen him fuming. By God, the girl was taking advantage of him, if he wasn't mistaken, and he didn't like it. Rosie was squatted in front of him. He came up groggy and paused a moment. Then he gave Rosie a very effective kick that sent her sprawling. Rosie jumped up and smacked Rex in the mouth. The gang jumped in and tried to establish order.

It was agreed that the Leapfrog contest must not change into a fight. Not any more. Not with Fowler only five or ten minutes away. The gang ruled further that Rex had had no right to kick Rosie and that in smacking him in the mouth Rosie had squared the matter, and the contest was to continue.

Rosie was very tired and sore; and so was Rex. They began leaping and squatting again; and again we saw Rosie coming down on Rex's neck so that his head was bumping the ground.

It looked pretty bad for the boy from Texas. We couldn't understand how he could take so much punishment. We all felt that Rex was getting what he had coming to him, but at the same time everybody seemed to feel badly about Rosie, a girl, doing the job instead of one of us. Of course, that was where we were wrong. Nobody but Rosie could have figured out that smart way of humiliating a very powerful and superior boy. It was probably the woman in her, which, less than five years later, came out to such an extent that she became one of the most beautiful girls in town, gave up tomboy activities, and married one of the wealthiest young men in Kings County, a college man named, if memory serves, Wallace Hadington Finlay VI.

Less than a hundred yards from the heart of Fowler, Rosie, with great and admirable artistry, finished the job.

That was where the dirt of the highway siding ended and the paved main street of Fowler began. This street was paved with cement, not asphalt. Asphalt, in that heat, would have been too soft to serve, but cement had exactly the right degree of brittleness. I think Rex, when he squatted over the hard cement, knew the game was up. But he was brave to the end. He squatted over the hard cement and waited for the worst. Behind him, Rosie Mahoney prepared to make the supreme effort. In this next leap, she intended to give her all, which she did.

She came down on Rex Folger's neck like a ton of bricks. His head banged against the hard cement, his body straightened out, and his arms and legs twitched.

He was out like a light.

Six paces in front of him, Rosie Mahoney squatted and waited. Jim Telesco counted twenty, which was the time allowed for each leap. Rex didn't get up during the count.

The contest was over. The winner of the contest was Rosie Mahoney.

Rex didn't get up by himself at all. He just stayed where he was until a half-dozen of us lifted him and carried him to a horse trough, where we splashed water on his face.

Rex was a confused young man all the way back. He was also a deeply humiliated one. He couldn't understand anything about anything. He just looked dazed and speechless. Every now and then we imagined he wanted to talk, and I guess he did, but after we'd all gotten ready to hear what he had to say, he couldn't speak. He made a gesture so tragic that tears came to the eyes of eleven members of the gang.

Rosie Mahoney, on the other hand, talked all the way home. She said everything.

I think it made a better man of Rex. More human. After that he was a gentler sort of soul. It may have been because he couldn't see very well for some time. At any rate, for weeks he seemed to be going around in a dream. His gaze would freeze on some insignificant object far away in the landscape, and half the time it seemed as if he didn't know where he was going, or why. He took little part in the activities of the gang, and the following winter he stayed away altogether. He came to school one day wearing glasses. He looked broken and pathetic.

That winter Rosie Mahoney stopped hanging around with the gang, too. She had a flair for making an exit at the right time.

The Brothers and the Sisters

Brother Matthew from Tennessee was the youngest of the Brothers. He was like any man, not like a churchman. The other Brothers were fond of him, but felt superior. They were all professors of this and that and the other thing. As far as the young man Jack Towey was concerned, they were bores.

Jack Towey was twenty-one and very big. One day he lifted Brother Garcia off the floor and held him overhead. Brother Garcia was a very dignified man who weighed around one hundred and fifty pounds. The young man did not lift Brother Garcia off the floor until Brother Garcia had given him permission to do so.

Brother Garcia, the young man had said, do you know I can lift you off the floor and hold you overhead?

Brother Garcia was, of course, somewhat stunned.

No, he said. I've never given it a thought.

I can, Jack Towey said. Will you let me?

If you wish, Brother Garcia said.

I won't hurt you, the young man said.

Lord in Heaven, Brother Garcia said, I believe you. Please let me down.

It's easy for me, the young man said. I won't drop you. I could hold you up this way for an hour, I guess.

I'd rather you let me down, Brother Garcia said.

The young man put the Brother on the floor extra gently, as if the Brother were something that might break if jarred.

The others were eating lunch in the sunlight, sitting outside on the steps of the building. The young man wasn't with them because Brother Matthew was out of town. Brother Garcia had stayed upstairs during the lunch hour in the hope of doing some reading. After the young man had lifted him and let him down Brother Garcia felt strangely dissatisfied with himself. He felt that he ought to exercise more and develop his body. There was some dignity in having one's spirit housed in strong substance. He rather envied the young man's strength.

All right, he said. You'll have to excuse me now. I have some reading to do.

Don't you get tired of reading all the time? the young man said.

I don't read all the time, Brother Garcia said.

Brother Garcia sat down with his book. The young man went to the window where he remained standing for some time.

Brother Garcia lifted his eyes from the book now and then to watch the young man.

Brother Garcia, the boy said.

Yes? the Brother said.

Have you noticed the hotel across the street?

I know it's there, the Brother said. What about it?

Brother Garcia knew all about the hotel across the street. All the Brothers knew about it. It was one of many places of its kind in the North Beach.

I think they've got some girls upstairs, the young man said.

Is that so? the Brother said.

I think so, the young man said. Every day I've seen men come and go. Have you ever seen any of the girls?

I don't believe I have, the Brother said.

I saw one of them yesterday evening, the young man said. She was just a kid. That's what I can't understand.

What do you mean? the Brother said.

I mean, the young man said, why didn't she marry some young fellow instead? There are a lot of young fellows who'd like to marry a girl like her if they knew she was a good girl. She was very pretty. If you weren't a Brother, Brother Garcia, and you liked a girl like her, would you marry her anyway?

I don't know, the Brother said.

It sure surprised me when I saw how young and pretty she was, the young man said. She looked like a good girl. If I hadn't seen her come out of the hotel. I would have believed she was a good girl. She smiled at me. I'd hate to fall in love with a girl like her.

Yes, the Brother said, that would only make you unhappy.

I feel unhappy now, the young man said. I'm not in love with her or anything, but it makes me sore to think she'd love anybody who'd pay for it. Have you ever gone up to any of those places?

Lord in Heaven, no, the Brother said.

I mean just to look around, the young man said. Maybe a Brother could do something about it.

I'm afraid not, the Brother said.

I don't know, the young man said, but I've got a feeling I ought to do something.

What could you do? the Brother said.

I don't know, the young man said, but I've got a feeling I ought to do something. It don't seem right.

After lunch the Brothers came upstairs and went on with their work. The only other worker in the winery who was not a Brother was old Angelo Fanucci. He worked with the young man, Jack Towey. He was a small man of fifty-seven whose life had been ruined by an unfortunate event of many years ago.

Angelo, the young man would say, did you see the fleet come in?

What do I care about the fleet? the old man would say. Will it go to the Bank of Italy and get my *tirteen tousand* dollars?

It was the same with everything.

Angelo, the young man would say, have you walked across the Golden Gate Bridge?

Why should I walk across the bridge? the old man would say. On the other side will I find my *tirteen tousand* dollars? Some day I will get that woman.

Then he would swear violently in Italian.

After work that evening the young man stayed in the winery until all the Brothers had gone home. The janitor and night watchman, Louis Getas, noticed him standing at the window.

Why you no go home? he said.

I'll be going in a little while, the young man said.

What you looking? the janitor said.

Nothing, the young man said.

He saw a man hurry into the doorway, press the button, and a moment later turn the knob of the door, open it, and hurry upstairs.

He felt a great hatred for the man because he was afraid the man might choose the girl he had seen yesterday and for a moment he wanted to go across the street, upstairs, and throw the man out of the place.

The following day Brother Matthew returned to the winery from the country. He had arranged to purchase many tons of wine grapes from vineyardists of the San Joaquin valley.

The young man was glad to see him back. When he was

alone with the Brother he said, Brother Matthew, you know about this place across the street.

Sure, the young Brother said. Don't tell me you want to take me up there with you to spend some money.

The young man laughed. It was pleasant to talk with a Brother like Brother Matthew.

I'd like to go up there, the young man said.

Well, said Brother Matthew, for all I know maybe I would, too, but I'm not going to.

I don't mean to spend money, the young man said. There's a girl up there I'd like to talk to.

What do you want to talk to her for? the Brother said.

Well, I don't think she should be in a place like that, the young man said. It burns me up.

Who is this girl? the Brother said.

I don't know, the young man said. I saw her in the street a couple of days ago. Do you think maybe you could go up there with me?

What do you want to talk to her about? the Brother said.

I don't want her to stay in a place like that, the young man said.

I don't believe the girl would be interested in hearing that kind of talk, the Brother said.

She smiled at me, the young man said.

It may be, the Brother said, that she smiles at every man. It is possible that she would even smile at me. You're not in love with her, are you?

I've never been in love, the young man said. I don't know how it feels to be in love. I feel sore at everybody. What I want to know is what kind of a world is this when a girl like that has to be in a place like that? Will you go up there with me tonight after work?

Why don't you forget you ever saw her? the Brother said.

I guess I ought to, the young man said, but ever since I . her I've felt sore at everybody.

Why don't you go up alone? the Brother said.

I'm afraid to go up alone, the young man said.

What are you afraid of? the Brother said.

I don't know, the young man said. If you go with me, I'll feel better.

The Brother thought it over a moment.

All right, he said. I hope nobody sees us. We'll have to be very careful.

That evening after work the young man and Brother Matthew took a walk until it was dark. Then they returned to the winery and when nobody was in sight they hurried across the street to the doorway of the hotel and the Brother pressed the button. Each of them was frightened.

Shall we go up? the young man asked the Brother.

There's still time to go away, the Brother said. Perhaps we'd better.

They heard the electric lock buzz. The Brother took the door knob and opened the door two or three inches.

Somebody's coming down the street, the young man said.

The Brother pushed the door open and the two young men hurried up the stairs.

There was a nauseating odor of powder and perfume in the place. At the top of the stairs was a middle-aged woman in a green tight-fitting dress with no sleeves.

Good evening, boys, she said.

Good evening, Brother Matthew replied.

When the woman noticed the Brother's clothes, she smiled.

She led the young men to a waiting-room. They did not sit down.

I've always wondered what the inside of one of these places was like, the Brother said.

It wasn't much unlike any other small hotel, except for the way it made you feel. The odor of the place and your knowing what kind of a place it was made you feel any number of ways at once. You felt ashamed and foolish and amused and sorrowful, but more than anything else you felt that living was an ugly thing, and then because you knew this was so you felt the absurdity of trying to be good and you wondered if living the heedless life wasn't more true and real than living the good one.

When the girls came into the room they saw two excited young men, one of them a Catholic Brother. This embarrassed the girls and brought to an end something in them which was an essential part of their work, a partly-artificial and partly-genuine mood of gaiety, daring, recklessness, and good-humor. They became inwardly and outwardly clumsy. The innocence in the girls returned in them to meet the same thing in the young men. They were like three sisters. The young Brother's momentary feeling of wickedness fell away from him and instead of being excited by the girls as he had imagined he might be he felt more truly immune to sin than ever before in his life. He was, in fact, rather delighted that he had come.

The young man, however, could not take his eyes away from the girl who had smiled at him. Now, in this place, she did not smile, and he tried to understand this. He seemed to feel that what she had shared with him in the street was a thing which did not come with her to this place, a thing which nothing could take away from her, and which needed no guarding.

The Brother looked at each of the girls and then at the young man, asking with his glance if the young man wished to talk to the girl. The young man answered with an almost imperceptible shaking of his head.

The young Brother felt strangely happy.

We work in the winery across the street, he said at last. My friend and I thought we'd come in and say hello and ask if might bring you some wine.

This broke down the feeling of awkwardness in everyone. The girls and the young men began to talk and laugh. The young men offered the girls cigarettes and every one but the girl who had smiled at the young man smoked. The young man asked the girl if she'd like to go for a walk with him some evening and she said perhaps she would. This made him very happy.

The Brother and the young man promised to return soon with wine, and then went away.

In the street the two young men felt lively, but at the same time, for some reason, deeply sorrowful.

They're wonderful people, aren't they? the young man said.

Yes, they are, the Brother said. I don't believe I've ever met such truly innocent people.

I want to thank you for going with me, the young man said. If I didn't go, I'd feel bad all the time.

I'm glad you asked me to go, the Brother said.

They hurried along the street in silence for two blocks, and then suddenly the young man wanted to vomit. He began to cry, and the Brother, for the first time in his life, understood how difficult living would always have to be for everybody.

The Vision

Kyrie eleison, said the priest. *Kyrie eleison,* answered the clerk. *Kyrie eleison,* said the priest again. *Christe eleison,* said the clerk. *Christe eleison,* answered the priest. *Christe eleison,* said the clerk again.

Et cum spiritu tuo, said the clerk.

Then he removed the massbook and knelt at the altar.

The priest said:

Dominus vobiscum.

Et cum spiritu tuo, answered the clerk.

The clerk was a young man of eighteen. The priest was a short old man of sixty who was growing fat and listless. The priest went through the mass as if he didn't have much faith in what he was doing, but the clerk served him humbly and with energy, giving the priest wine and water, preparing the basin and cloth, removing the basin and cloth when the priest had washed and dried his hands, kneeling and moving about, crying out humbly yet passionately the Latin words he had memorized but did not understand. The young man felt, nevertheless, that he was saying words of some importance and certainly of great dignity. *Et cum spiritu tuo,* he cried w youthful passion, and the priest felt dimly: This boy is an ox he bellows; he does not chant.

It was James Giordano. He was a new clerk at St. Anne's. He came from somewhere in the North Beach, and seemed to be a more than normally serious young man. The priest thought he would have a little talk with the boy some time soon and find out why he was so serious. Some of the Irish boys who served the priest were no less efficient than James Giordano, and yet they were more amusing to have around. They made him feel there was still liveliness and mischief in the living, and even when they forgot their lines or said them wrong or out of place, he didn't mind, and on the contrary smiled to himself, keeping, all the while, a most pious face.

The boy all but ran into the church only an evening later, and he was almost out of breath when he found the priest.

Father, he said, I want to talk to you. I don't want to confess because I haven't had any new sins since last confession. I only want to talk to somebody.

The priest walked with him out of the church. It was a clear winter evening.

And *I* want to talk to *you,* the priest said. We will take a little walk together.

They walked down Nineteenth Avenue towards the park.

Something is troubling you, the priest said.

Yes, Father, said the boy.

What is it, my boy?

Father, I have visions.

Visions? cried the priest. What do you mean?

And he thought: Now I begin to understand. I know these young men. Night and day they think of only one thing, and the serious ones are worse than the others. And in his mind he saw the young man dreaming all day and night of the great dy of woman, the gigantic female of the instincts. He would talk to the boy quietly. Find yourself a good companion, he would say. The Lord created you to share your life with another. There is no evil in love.

And rather than pity the boy, the priest envied him. Which way of life is holier than the simple and innocent way? he wondered. Unknowing, and in ignorance, they achieve godliness.

They walked in the park. The tall eucalyptus-trees made deep shadows and the stillness was soothing to the priest. It was good to be walking beside a young man, one who would soon enter life in all its fullness.

Tell me what you see, said the priest.

Father, said the boy, I see the world ending. For weeks now I have been seeing the end of the world. I am not frightened, but I want to talk to you.

This angered the priest. He was a man of little faith, and he did not believe it was possible for an ignorant young man, an Italian, to have such a terrible and glorious vision.

What happens? he said.

Father, said the boy, everything ends. The cities burn and fall, and the living die.

What nonsense, thought the priest.

I thought I ought to tell you, the boy said.

Well, said the priest, it is because you are young. There is nothing to fear.

Father, said the boy. He was very anxious.

Father, he said, I am not afraid for myself. I am prepared to die. I am afraid for the others who are not prepared, the worldful of them. They do not know. I thought I ought to tell you. I see the world ending all the time. When I close my eyes to sleep I see everything ending, and when I open my eyes I see all the people dying. I thought I ought to tell somebody.

The priest took the boy by the arm.

It is nothing, he said.

Nothing? the boy said.

It is all right, the priest said.

The boy did not understand. Father, he said, I see them dying. I thought somebody ought to tell them.

How old are you? the priest said.

I am eighteen, Father.

Have you a job?

Yes, Father. I am a waiter at the Fior D'Italia on Broadway.

Have you had a loss recently?

A loss, Father?

Has someone dear to you passed away? Your mother or father, a sister or a brother?

No, Father, they are all alive.

Have you a girl?

A girl, Father?

Are you in love?

No, Father.

I thought so, the priest thought.

He believed he had reached the bottom of the whole thing, and was quite pleased.

It is nothing, he said. There are many nice girls in the church, he said.

What shall I do, Father?

Find a good girl, the priest said.

Father, he said, do you mean that I should find a girl and tell her about the vision? Do you mean I should tell only one person to be prepared? Not all of them?

Good Lord, the priest thought.

Why do you feel you must tell everybody about the vision? he said.

I see the world ending, Father, he said. I see everybody dying.

Everyone alive will some day leave his mortal flesh, the priest said.

This dying is not the same, Father, the boy said. They go on moving around the same as ever, but there is death in them. I cannot explain it, Father. I see them dying all the time, and they *will* die.

Nonsense, the priest thought. What shall I tell him?

Oh, he said.

What shall I do? the boy said.

The priest himself wanted to know what *he* should do. The boy was certainly in earnest. He was certainly seeing the world ending and the living dying. He was not anyone sly or mischievous. He was not playing a joke.

The priest wondered what *he* would do if he were eighteen and very ignorant and very faithful and was having visions of the world ending and the living dying. It would be a very awkward experience, to say the least.

There is nothing to do, he said. You must be patient, and I think it would be very nice if you found a good Catholic girl.

They walked together in silence out of the park. The priest was not altogether pleased with himself because he knew the boy's vision was no common thing. If the truth were known, it was a most remarkable thing. But good Lord, what could he do about it? What could anyone do about it?

In the street the young man said, I thought I ought to tell you, Father.

You did right in telling me, the priest said.

I will be patient, the boy said.

That's right, the priest said.

I will find a good Catholic girl, Father, the boy said.

I think that would be very nice, the priest said.

Good night, Father, the boy said.

Good night, the priest said.

That was all. But walking away from the boy, the priest w deeply troubled, deeply angry with himself, but even mor deeply jealous of the boy. Who was he, a boy of eighteen, to have such a vision? It was ridiculous.

Ever Fall in Love with a Midget?

I don't suppose you ever fell in love with a midget weighing thirty-nine pounds, did you?

No, I said, but have another beer.

Down in Gallup, he said, twenty years ago. Fellow by the name of Rufus Jenkins came to town with six white horses and two black ones. Said he wanted a man to break the horses for him because his left leg was wood and he couldn't do it. Had a meeting at Parker's Mercantile Store and finally came to blows, me and Henry Walpal. Bashed his head with a brass cuspidor and ran away to Mexico, but he didn't die.

Couldn't speak a word. Took up with a cattle-breeder named Diego, educated in California. Spoke the language better than you and me. Said, Your job, Murph, is to feed them prize bulls. I said, Fine; what'll I feed them? He said, Hay, lettuce, salt, and beer. I said, Fine; they're your bulls.

Came to blows two days later over an accordion he claimed I stole. I borrowed it and during the fight busted it over his head; ruined one of the finest accordions I ever saw. Grabbed a horse and rode back across the border. Texas. Got to talking with a fellow who looked honest. Turned out to be a Ranger who was looking for me.

Yeah, I said. You were saying, a thirty-nine pound midget.

Will I ever forget that lady? he said. Will I ever get over that amazon of small proportions?

Will you? I said.

If I live to be sixty, he said.

Sixty? I said. You look more than sixty now.

That's trouble showing in my face. Trouble and complications. I was fifty-six three months ago.

Oh.

Told the Texas Ranger my name was Rothstein, mining engineer from Pennsylvania, looking for something worth while. Mentioned two places in Houston. Nearly lost an eye early one morning, going down the stairs. Ran into a six-footer with an iron-claw where his right hand was supposed to be. Said, You broke up my home. Told him I was a stranger in Houston. The girls gathered at the top of the stairs to see a fight. Seven of them. Six feet and an iron-claw. That's bad on the nerves. Kicked him in the mouth when he swung for my head with the claw. Would have lost an eye except for quick thinking. Rolled into the gutter and pulled a gun. Fired seven times, but I was back upstairs. Left the place an hour later, dressed in silk and feathers, with a hat swung around over my face. Saw him standing on the corner, waiting. Said, Care for a wiggle? Said he didn't. Went on down the street, left town.

I don't suppose you ever had to put on a dress to save your skin, did you?

No, I said, and I never fell in love with a midget weighing thirty-nine pounds. Have another beer.

Thanks. Ever try to herd cattle on a bicycle?

No, I said.

Left Houston with sixty cents in my pocket, gift of a girl

named Lucinda. Walked fourteen miles in fourteen hours. Big house with barb-wire all around, and big dogs. One thing I never could get around. Walked past the gate, anyway, from hunger and thirst. Dogs jumped up and came for me. Walked right into them, growing older every second. Went up to the door and knocked. Big negress opened the door, closed it quick. Said, On your way, white trash.

Knocked again. Said, On your way. Again. On your way. Again. This time the old man himself opened the door, ninety if he was a day. Sawed-off shotgun too.

Said, I ain't looking for trouble, Father. I'm hungry and thirsty, name's Cavanaugh.

Took me in and made mint juleps for the two of us.

Said, Living here alone, Father?

Said, Drink and ask no questions; maybe I am and maybe I ain't. You saw the negress. Draw your own conclusions.

I'd heard of that, but didn't wink out of tact.

Called out, Elvira, bring this gentleman sandwiches.

Young enough for a man of seventy, probably no more than forty, and big.

Said, Any good at cards? Said, No.

Said, Fine, Cavanaugh, take a hand of poker.

Played all night.

If I told you that old Southern gentleman was my grandfather, you wouldn't believe, would you?

No.

Well, it so happens he wasn't, although it would have been remarkable if he had been.

Where did you herd cattle on a bicycle?

Toledo, Ohio, 1918.

Toledo, Ohio? I said. They don't herd cattle up there.

They don't any more. They did in 1918. One fellow did, leastways. Bookkeeper named Sam Gold. Only Jewish cowboy

I ever saw. Straight from the Eastside New York. Sombrero, lariats, Bull Durham, two head of cattle, and two bicycles. Called his place Gold Bar Ranch, two acres, just outside the city limits.

That was the year of the War, you'll remember.

Yeah, I said.

Remember a picture called *Shoulder Arms?*

Sure. Saw it five times.

Remember when Charlie Chaplin thought he was washing *his* foot, and the foot turned out to be another man's?

Sure.

You may not believe me, but I was the man whose foot was washed by Chaplin in that picture.

It's possible, I said, but how about herding them two cows on a bicycle? How'd you do it?

Easiest thing in the world. Rode no hands. Had to, otherwise couldn't lasso the cows. Worked for Sam Gold till the cows ran away. Bicycles scared them. They went into Toledo and we never saw hide or hair of them again. Advertised in every paper, but never got them back. Broke his heart. Sold both bikes and returned to New York.

Took four aces from a deck of red cards and walked to town. Poker. Fellow in the game named Chuck Collins, liked to gamble. Told him with a smile I didn't suppose he'd care to bet a hundred dollars I wouldn't hold four aces the next hand. Called it. My cards were red on the blank side. The other cards were blue. Plumb forgot all about it. Showed him four aces. Ace of spades, ace of clubs, ace of diamonds, ace of hearts. I'll remember them four cards if I live to be sixty. Would have been killed on the spot except for the hurricane that year.

Hurricane?

You haven't forogotten the Toledo hurricane of 1918, have you?

No, I said. There was no hurricane in Toledo, in 1918, or any other year.

For the love of God, then, what do you suppose that commotion was? And how come I came to Chicago? Dream-walking down State Street?

I guess they scared you.

No, that wasn't it. You go back to the papers of November, 1918, and I think you'll find there was a hurricane in Toledo. I remember sitting on the roof of a two-story house, floating northwest.

Northwest?

Sure.

Okay, have another beer.

Thanks, he said, thaaaaanks.

I don't suppose *you* ever fell in love with a midget weighing thirty-nine pounds, did you? I said.

Who? he said.

You? I said.

No, he said, can't say I have.

Well, I said, let *me* tell *you* about it.

Dear Baby

The room was a large one on the seventh floor of the Blackstone Hotel on O'Farrell Street in San Francisco. There was nothing in it to bring him there except the portable radio-phonograph, the one record, and darkness.

He came into the room smiling, and walked about, trying to decide what to do. He had six hours to go, and after that a time so long he didn't like to think about it.

He no longer saw the room. During the day the blind of the only window was drawn to keep the place dark. At night he turned the light of the bathroom on and kept the door almost shut so that only enough light came into the room to keep him from walking into something. It happened anyway. It wasn't that he couldn't see as well as ever. It was simply that he was alone again all the time and wasn't looking. There was no longer any reason to look.

He remembered everything.

At the core of everything was his remembrance of her.

He walked about quietly, turning, bumping into the edges of doorways and chairs and other objects in the room, moving unconsciously, his eyes unable to see because of the remembrance. He stopped suddenly, removed his hat and coat, stretched and shook his head as he did when he was confused in the ring.

It was nothing.

He could go on as if he had never known her. He could be boisterous in act and loud in laughter, and some day be all right again. He could go on like everybody else in the world, but he didn't know if he wanted to. Lazzeri said he was in better shape than ever, but Lazzeri didn't know what he knew.

The odor of her hair, the taste of her mouth, and the image of her face came to him. His guts sickened. He smiled and sat on the bed. After a moment he got up, went to the portable machine, turned the knob, and put needle to disc. Then he stretched out on the bed, face down, and listened to the music, remembering her, and saying: "Dear baby, remembering you is the only truth I know. Having known you is the only beauty of my life. In my heart, there is one smile, the smile of your heart when we were together."

When the telephone rang he knew it was Lazzeri. He got up and turned off the machine.

"Joe?" Lazzeri said.

"Yeah."

"Are you all right?"

"Sure."

"Remember what I told you?"

"What did you tell me?"

"I want you to take it easy."

"That's what I'm doing."

"Don't go haywire."

"O.K."

"What's the matter?"

"I've been sleeping."

"Oh," Lazzeri said. "O.K. I'll see you at nine."

"O.K."

"Something's the matter," Lazzeri said.

"Don't be silly."

"Something's the matter," Lazzeri said again. "I'm coming right up."

"I've been sleeping," Joe said. "I'll see you at nine."

"You don't sound right," Lazzeri said.

"I'm fine."

"You haven't got somebody in that room with you, have you?"

"No."

"Joe," Lazzeri said, "what's the matter?"

"I'll see you at nine," Joe said.

"You're not going haywire on me again, are you?"

"No."

"O.K.," Lazzeri said. "If you're all right, that's all I want to know."

"I'm all right," Joe said.

"O.K.," Lazzeri said. "If you want to be alone, O.K. Just don't go haywire."

"I'll see you at nine," Joe said.

He went back to the machine, turned the knob, and then decided not to listen to the music any more. That's what he would do. He wouldn't listen to the music any more. He would break the record. He would give the machine away. He would lift the blind of the window. He would turn on all the lights and open his eyes. He would come to the room only to sleep. He would go down to the poolroom on Turk Street and find a couple of the boys. He would shoot pool and listen to the boys talking about cards and horses and the other varieties of trouble they knew. He would go up to a couple of the places he used to visit and find some girls he used to know and buy them drinks and ask how they'd been and hear them tell of the troubles *they* knew. He would stop being alone.

He began to laugh, at first quietly and then out loud. He laughed at himself—the wretched comedy of his grief. Then he laughed at everybody alive, and began to feel everything was going to be all right again. If you could laugh, you could live. If you could look at it that way, you could endure *anything*. While he was laughing he heard *her* laughing with him, as clearly as if she were in the room. He became sick again and stopped laughing, knowing it was no use.

He remembered her as if she were still alive, walking beside him along one of many streets in one of many cities, her face childlike and solemn, her movement beside him shy and full of innocence, her voice so young and lovely he would stop anywhere to hold her in his arms while she said seriously: "Joe, people are looking."

He remembered her alone with him in one of many rooms, her presence the first goodness and beauty in his life. He remembered the sweetness of her mouth and the soft hum of her heart growing to the sudden sobbing that brought out in him a tenderness so intense it was ferocious, a tenderness he had always hidden because there had never been anyone to give it to.

He walked about in the dark room, remembering how unkind he had been to her the night he had come home and found her listening to the record. He pointed at the machine and said, "Where did that come from?"

He remembered the way she ran to him and put her arms around him and the way he pushed her away. He remembered the way she moved away from him and said, "I only made a down payment on it. I'll tell them to come and take it back if you want me to. I thought you'd like it."

The record was playing, and although he knew it was something he liked very much, and needed, and should have known long ago, he went on being unkind. She was on the verge of crying and didn't know where to go or what to do. She went timidly to the machine and was going to shut it off when he shouted at her to let it play. She hurried, almost ran, into the other room, and he stood in front of the machine with his hat on and listened to the record until it finished. Then he shut off the machine and went back to town and didn't come home till after five in the morning. She was asleep. He couldn't understand what right he had to know her, to speak to her, to live in the same house with her, to touch her. He bent over her and touched her lips with his own and saw her eyes open. "Please forgive me," he said.

She sat up smiling and put her arms around him, and he kissed her lips and her nose and her eyes and her ears and her forehead and her neck and her shoulders and her arms and her hands, and while he was doing so he said, "Please remember one thing, baby. No matter what I say to you, I love you. I'm liable to go haywire any time, but don't forget that I love you. Please remember that."

He took off his clothes, got into his bed and went to sleep. When she got in beside him he woke up and embraced her, laughing, while she whispered his name the sorrowful, serious way she always did when she knew he was all right again.

That was in Ventura, where they had taken an apartment because he had three fights coming up in that vicinity: one in Los Angeles, one in Hollywood, and one in Pismo Beach. He let her come to the fight in Hollywood the night he fought Kid Fuente, the Indian, because he knew how much she wanted to see him in the ring. He got her a ringside seat and after the fight she told him she had sat next to Robert Taylor and Barbara Stanwyck and they had been very nice to her.

"I hope you didn't ask them for an autograph," he said, and she became embarrassed and said, "Yes, I did, Joe."

"Well," he said, "they should have asked *you* for one."

"Oh, they were swell," she said. "They sure liked you."

"Oh, sure," he said. "Sure. Sure. That dumb Indian almost ruined me. I don't know how I won. I guess he got tired trying. I'll be punch-drunk in another three or four months."

"You were wonderful in the ring," the girl said.

He remembered the fight because she had talked about it so much. It was six rounds. He was almost out in the fourth. She had known it and kept talking around it, but one day she said, "I almost cried."

"What are you talking about?" he said.

"I mean," she said, "at the fight. Everybody was yelling and I didn't know whether they were for you or against you and I almost cried."

"When was that?" he said.

"I don't know," she said. "I was so excited. He was fighting hard and you were in a corner and everybody stood up and was yelling. I thought he was hitting *me*."

He remembered being in the corner, taking a lot of bad ones, not being able to do anything about them, not knowing if he wasn't going to be out and saying to himself, "You'll be punch-drunk in no time at this rate." He kept trying to move away, but there was nowhere to go, and all of a sudden the Indian slowed down, he was tired, and he remembered saying to the Indian, "O.K., Kid, that's all." He knew he was going to be all right now because there weren't more than fifteen seconds to that round. He gave the rest of the round everything he had. The Indian was tired and couldn't do anything, and just before the bell the Indian stopped a bad one and fell backward, looking up at him with an amazed expression because the Indian couldn't understand how anybody could take so much punishment and come up so strong.

The bell saved the Indian, but for the rest of the fight the

Indian was no good, and he knocked him down once in each of the last two rounds.

"That was a bad spot," he told her. "By rights I should have been out, but the Indian got tired. You can't start slugging that way in the middle of a round and expect to keep it up till the end of the round."

"You looked fine," she said, "and you didn't look sore. Don't you get sore?"

"Sore?" he said. "Who's there to get sore at? That poor Indian is only out to earn a little money, the same as me. He's got nothing against me and I've got nothing against him. If he can floor me, he's going to do it, and if I can floor him, I'm going to do it."

"Well," she said, "I almost cried. You looked so fine all the rest of the fight, but when you were in the corner the only thing I could see was somebody being hit over and over again."

"I didn't like that myself," he said.

He was glad she hadn't seen some of his bad fights—the earlier ones, the ones in which he had taken a lot of punishment. Lately he'd learned enough about the racket not to get into a lot of trouble. He seldom took advantage of a chance to clinch, but if the worst came to the worst and there was nothing else to do he would do it, rest a few seconds and try to figure out what to do in the remaining seconds of the round. He usually ended every round nicely, coming back if he had been hurt earlier. Of course he had the reach, his legs were good, and even when he was hurt they didn't wobble and he could stay solid.

After seeing the fight with Kid Fuente she didn't want to see any more. The day of a fight she would be sick, sick in bed, and she would pray. She would turn on the phonograph and listen to the record, which had become their music, the song of their life together. And when he'd come home he'd find her pale and sick and almost in tears, listening to the song. He would hold her in his arms a long time, and he would hear her heart pounding, and little by little it would slow down to almost normal, and then he would hold her at arm's length and look into her eyes and she would be smiling and then he would say, "It only means fifty dollars extra, baby, but I won." And she'd know there was no vanity in him, she'd understand what he was talking about, and she would ask him what she could get him. Ham and eggs? Scotch and soda? What would he like? She would rush around in an apron and fool around with food and dishes and put the stuff on the table.

He used to eat even if he wasn't hungry. Just so he hadn't lost. If he'd lost, he'd be mean, he'd be so sore at himself that he'd be mean to her, and she wouldn't know what to do, but in the midst of being mean to her he would suddenly say in a loud voice, "And don't be a fool, either; don't pay any attention to anything I'm saying now because I'm out of my head. I made a mess of the whole fight."

When he came home from the fight with Sammy Kaufman of New York he was pretty badly hurt. His head was heavy, his lips were swollen, his left eye was twitching, every muscle of his body was sore, and he was swearing all the time, even though it had been a good fight and a draw.

He wasn't mean to her that night, though, and she said, "Joe, please give it up. You can make money some other way. We don't need a lot of money."

He walked around the apartment and talked to himself. Then suddenly he calmed down and shut off the lights and put the record on the machine and sat down with her to listen to their song. It was a piece by Jan Sibelius, from the *King Kristian Suite,* called "Elegie." He played the record three times, then fell asleep from exhaustion, and she kept playing the record until he woke up a half-hour later. He was smiling, and he said, "I'd like to quit, baby, but I don't know any other way to make money."

The following week he tried gambling and lost.

After that he had stuck to fighting. They had traveled together up and down the coast—north to San Francisco, Sacramento, Reno, Portland, and Seattle, and then south to the towns along the coast and in the valley that were good fight towns, and Hollywood and Los Angeles and San Diego—when he found out about it. From the beginning he was scared to death, in spite of how good it made him feel. He tried his best not to be scared and tried to keep her in good spirits, but he was worried about it all the time. She was a child herself. She was too little. He didn't know what to do. He remembered her saying one night, "Please let me have it, Joe. I want it so badly."

"Do you think I don't want it?" he said. "Do you think I don't want you to have it? That's *all* I want. That's all I've ever wanted."

Then he began to mumble, talking to himself.

"What, Joe?" she said.

"Do you feel all right?" he said. "Do you feel you can do it? You're not scared, are you?"

"I'm a little scared," she said, "but I guess everybody's scared the first time."

The months of waiting were the happiest of his life. Everything that was good in him had come out—even though he was worried all the time. Even in the ring he had been better than ever. His fights were all good, except one, and that was the fight with the champion, Corbett, which had been a draw, but very close, some sports writers saying he had won and others saying that Corbett had won, and everybody wanting a rematch, especially Lazzeri.

So tonight he was fighting Corbett again. He had six hours to go. If he won this fight he and Lazzeri would be in the big money at last. He believed he could take the fight, but what if he did? What did he care about money now? Suppose he did take the fight? Where could he go *after* the fight?

"I'm dead," he said. "What's the use bluffing?"

Remembering the girl, he fell asleep, and when he woke up he went to the telephone, without thinking, and asked the hotel operator to get him Corbett at Ryan's Gymnasium, and call him back. A moment later the telephone rang. He answered it, and Corbett said, "Hello, is that you, Joe?"

"Ralph," Joe said, "I want to tell you I'm out to win tonight. I think it's about time you retired."

At the other end of the line Corbett busted out laughing and swore at his friend in Italian.

"I'll take care of you, kid," he said. "You know I like an aggressive fighter."

"Don't say I didn't tell you," Joe said.

"See you in the ring," Corbett said.

In the ring, when they shook hands, Joe said, "This is going to be your last fight." Corbett didn't know he was talking to himself.

"O.K., Joe," he said.

The first round was fast and wild. Even the sports writers couldn't understand. Lazzeri was sore as hell.

"Joe," he said, "what do you think you're doing? You can't beat Corbett that way. Take it easy. Fight *his* fight."

The second round was faster and wilder than the first. They were probably even, but that was only because he wasn't tired yet. The music was humming in him all the time, getting into the roar of the crowd and sweeping along in him, while his heart kept talking to the girl, dreaming that she was still alive, at home listening to their song, waiting for him to come home and take her in his arms.

Lazzeri wanted to hit him after the second round. "Joe," he said, "listen to me. Fight Corbett's fight. He'll kill you."

("That's O.K. with me," his heart said. "Dear Baby, that's O.K. with me.")

The third round, if anything, was faster than the first and second, and coming out of a clinch Corbett said, "What do you think you're doing, Joe?"

"I'm knocking you out," Joe said.

Corbett laughed at him and they began slugging again, one for one, with the sports writers looking at each other, trying to figure out what was going on.

Lazzeri was furious.

"Joe," he said, "I'm not talking to you. I've worked with you six years. I changed you from a punk to a great fighter. Now you're throwing away the championship—the chance we've been working for all these years. You can go to hell, Joe. I hope he floors you in the next round."

During the fourth round things began to go haywire. Corbett's left eye was cut and bleeding badly, and it seemed he was bewildered and less strong than he had been.

("What the hell," his heart said. "Is Corbett going to go haywire at a time like this?")

After the round Lazzeri said, "Joe, I think you've got him—but I'll talk to you later. Your next fight will be in Madison Square Garden. We'll go to Florida for a while. But I'll talk to you later."

In the fifth round Corbett was slow, his punches were weak and he seemed confused. Toward the end of the round he fell and stayed on one knee to the count of nine.

"You're fighting the most beautiful fight you've ever fought," Lazzeri said. "The sports writers are crazy about you. You're a real champion, Joe."

The fight was stopped near the end of the sixth round because Corbett's eye was so bad.

Lazzeri was crazy with joy but unable to understand what had happened. It was obvious that Joe had fought a great fight—that his style had been perfect for *this* fight. And yet Lazzeri knew something was wrong somewhere.

"Joe," he said in the cab, "you're a champion now. What's eating you?"

"I'm not fighting for three or four months, am I?" he said.

"Two or three, anyway," Lazzeri said. "Why?"

"We've got more money than we've ever had before, haven't we?"

"We've got enough for both of us for two years at least," Lazzeri said. "But why? What are you driving at?"

"Nothing," he said. ("Dear Baby," his heart said.) "I think I'm entitled to a little celebrating."

"Sure, sure," Lazzeri said. "I don't want you to go stale. What do you want?"

"I want laughs," he said. "I'll go up to my room. Get a couple of girls. Bring some Scotch. I want *laughs*."

"Sure," Lazzeri said. "Sure, Joe. We'll have a little party. I need laughs myself after the scare you gave me."

When he got to his room he turned on all the lights, took the record off the phonograph, and for a moment thought of breaking it. He couldn't, though. He put the record under the bed, as if to hide it. He walked around the room until the sickness caught up with him again, only now it was worse than ever, and he sat down on the bed and began to cry.

When Lazzeri and the two girls came into the room it was dark except for a little light coming from the bathroom. The phonograph was playing, and the fighter was sitting on the bed with his head in his hands and he was crying.

"Get the hell out of here," he said softly.

Without a word Lazzeri led the two girls out of the room. "He'll be all right," he said.

"Dear Baby," the fighter kept saying over and over again.

The Declaration of War

On the 3rd of September 1939 a boy by the name of John came running into the barber shop on Moraga Avenue where I was getting a haircut.

"War's been declared in Europe," he said.

Mr. Tagalavia dropped the comb from one hand and the scissors from the other.

"You get out of this shop," he said. "I told you before."

"What's your name?" I said to the young man.

"John," he said.

"How old are you?" I said.

"Eleven," John said.

"You get out of this shop," Mr. Tagalavia said.

I was under the impression that Mr. Tagalavia was talking to John, but apparently he wasn't. He was talking to me. He wasn't talking to *himself*.

John had left the shop.

The barber untied his apron and threw it aside.

"Who?" I said.

"You," Mr. Tagalavia said.

"Why?"

"I try to run a respectable barber shop."

"I'm respectable."

"You talked to that foolish boy," the barber said. "I don't want people like you to come to my shop."

"He didn't *seem* foolish," I said.

"He is a foolish, foolish boy," the barber said. "I don't want foolish people to come here."

"I suppose it *was* a little foolish of me to ask the boy his name," I said. "I'm sorry about that. I'm a writer, you see, and I'm *always* asking people questions. I apologize. Please finish my haircut."

"No," the barber said. "That's all."

I got out of the chair and examined my head. My haircut was less than half finished. The shape of my head wasn't exactly what it might be, but I could always walk three or four blocks and have the job finished by an ordinary barber. I put on my tie and coat.

"Excuse me," I said. "How much do I owe you?"

"Nothing," the barber said. "I don't want money from people like you. If I starve—if my family starves—all right. No money from foolish people."

"I'm sorry," I said, "but I believe I owe you *something*. How about thirty-five cents?"

"Not a penny," the barber said. "Please go away. I will make a present of the haircut to you. I *give* to people. I do not take. I am a man, not a fool."

I suppose I should have left the shop at this point, but I felt quite sure that what he *really* wanted to do was talk.

I have a power of understanding which is greater than the average, and at times uncanny. I sense certain things which other people, for one reason or another, are unable to sense. (Sometimes what I sense is wrong and gets me in trouble, but I usually manage to get out of it. A kind word. A friendly tone of voice. A worldly attitude about such things. We are all brothers. The end is death for each of us. Let us love one another and try not to get excited.)

I sensed now that the barber was troubled or irritated; that he wished to speak and be heard; that, in fact, unless I missed my guess, his message was for *the world.* Traveling thousands of miles he could not have found anyone more prepared to listen to the message or to relay it to the world.

"Cigarette?" I said.

"I don't want anything," the barber said.

"Can I help you with the towels?"

"You get out of my shop."

Here, obviously, was an equal if I had ever encountered one. I have at times been spoken of by certain women who follow the course of contemporary literature as enigmatic and unpredictable, but after all I am a writer. One expects a writer to be impressive along the lines of enigma, and so on, but with barbers one usually expects a haircut or a shave or both, along with a little polite conversation, and nothing more. Women who have time to read are likely to believe that it is natural for a writer to have certain little idiosyncracies, but perhaps the only man in the world who can allow a *barber* similar privileges is a writer.

There is little pride in writers. They know they are human and shall some day die and be forgotten. We come, and go, and we are forgotten. Knowing all this a writer is gentle and kindly where another man is severe and unkind.

I decided to offer the barber the *full* cost of a haircut. Sixty-five cents, instead of thirty-five. A man can always get a haircut. There are more important things than making sure one has not been swindled.

"Excuse me," I said. "I don't think it's fair to you for me not to pay. It's true that you haven't finished my haircut, but perhaps some other day. I live near by. We shall be seeing more of one another."

"You get out of my shop," the barber said. "I don't want people like you to come here. Don't come back. I have no time."

"What do you mean, people like me? I am a writer."

"I don't care what you are," Mr. Tagalavia said. "You talked to that foolish boy."

"A few words," I said. "I had no idea it would displease you. He seemed excited and eager to be recognized by someone."

"He is a foolish, foolish boy," the barber said.

"Why do you say that?" I said. "He seemed sincere enough."

"Why do I say that!" the barber said. "Because he *is* foolish. Every day now for six days he has been running into my shop and shouting, War! War! War!"

"I don't understand," I said.

"You don't understand!" the barber said. "War! I don't know who you are, but let me tell you something."

"My name is Donald Kennebec," I said. "You may have heard of me."

"My name is Nick Tagalavia," the barber said. "I have never heard of you."

He paused and looked me in the eye.

"War?" he said.

"Yes," I said.

"You are a fool," the barber said. "Let me tell you something," he went on. "There is no war! I am a barber. I do not like people who are foolish. The whole thing is a trick. They want to see if the people are still foolish. They *are*. The people are more foolish now than ever. The boy comes running in here and says, 'War's been declared in Europe', and you talk to him. You encourage him. Pretty soon he believes everything, like you."

The barber paused and looked at me very closely again. I took off my hat, so he could see how far he had gone with the haircut, and how much he had left unfinished.

"What do you write?" he said.

"Memoirs," I said.

"You are a fool," the barber said. "Why do you encourage the boy? He's going to have trouble enough without wars. Why do you say, 'How old are you'?"

"I thought he was rather bright," I said. "I just wanted him to know I was aware of it."

"I don't want people like you to come to my shop," the barber said.

"People like me?" I said. "I *hate* war."

"Shut up," the barber said. "The world is full of fools like you. You hate war, but in Europe there *is* a war?"

The implication here was a little too fantastic.

"Excuse me," I said. "*I* didn't start the war."

"You hate war," the barber said again. "They tell you there's a war in Europe, so you believe there's a war in Europe."

"I have no reason to believe there's peace in Europe," I said.

"You hate war," he said. "The paper comes out with the headline War. The boy comes running into the shop. War. You come in for a haircut. War. Everybody believes. The world is full of fools. How did you lose your hair?"

"Fever," I said.

"Fever!" the barber said. "You lost your hair because you're a fool. Electric clippers. Comb. Scissors. You've got no hair to cut. The whole thing is a trick. I don't want any more fools to come here and make me nervous. There is no war."

I had been right in sensing that the barber had had something to say and had wanted someone to say it to. I was quite pleased.

"You are a remarkable man," I said.

"Don't talk," the barber shouted. "I'm no foolish boy of eleven. I'm fifty-nine years old. I am a remarkable man! Newspapers. Maps. You've got no hair on your head. What am I supposed to cut? The boy comes running in. You can't sit still. 'War is declared in Europe,' he says. 'What's your name? How old are you?' What's the matter? Are you crazy?"

"I didn't mean to upset you," I said. "Let me pay you."

"Never," the barber said. "I don't want anything. That's no haircut. Not a penny. If a man with a head of hair comes in here and sits down, I will take the electric clippers and give him a haircut. The hair falls down on the floor. No trouble. No excitement. No foolishness. He gets out of the chair. His head is in good shape. Ears feel fine. Sixty-five cents. Thank you. Good-bye. The boy comes running in. I say, 'Get out of my shop.' The boy runs out. No trouble."

"*Other* barbers give me haircuts," I said.

"All right," he said. "Go to other barbers. Please go to other barbers. Remember one thing. There is no war. Don't go around spreading propaganda."

I was now satisfied that I had successfully gotten to the bottom of the man's irritation, and had obtained fresh and original material for a new memoir, so without another word, I sauntered out of the shop and down the street.

I feel that I have effectively utilized the material; that I have shaped it into a work which, if anything, will enhance my already considerable fame.

New Directions Paperbooks — a partial listing

Kaouther Adimi, Our Riches
Adonis, Songs of Mihyar the Damascene
César Aira, Artforum
An Episode in the Life of a Landscape Painter
Ghosts
Will Alexander, The Sri Lankan Loxodrome
Osama Alomar, The Teeth of the Comb
Guillaume Apollinaire, Selected Writings
Paul Auster, The Red Notebook
White Spaces
Ingeborg Bachmann, Malina
Honoré de Balzac, Colonel Chabert
Djuna Barnes, Nightwood
Charles Baudelaire, The Flowers of Evil*
Bei Dao, City Gate, Open Up
Mei-Mei Berssenbrugge, Empathy
Max Blecher, Adventures in Immediate Irreality
Roberto Bolaño, By Night in Chile
Distant Star
Jorge Luis Borges, Labyrinths
Seven Nights
Coral Bracho, Firefly Under the Tongue*
Kamau Brathwaite, Ancestors
Basil Bunting, Complete Poems
Anne Carson, Glass, Irony & God
Norma Jeane Baker of Troy
Horacio Castellanos Moya, Senselessness
Camilo José Cela, Mazurka for Two Dead Men
Louis-Ferdinand Céline
Death on the Installment Plan
Journey to the End of the Night
Rafael Chirbes, On the Edge
Inger Christensen, alphabet
Julio Cortázar, All Fires the Fire
Cronopios & Famas
Jonathan Creasy, ed: Black Mountain Poems
Robert Creeley, If I Were Writing This
Guy Davenport, 7 Greeks
Osamu Dazai, No Longer Human
H.D., Selected Poems
Helen DeWitt, The Last Samurai
Some Trick
Marcia Douglas
The Marvellous Equations of the Dread
Daša Drndić, EEG
Robert Duncan, Selected Poems
Eça de Queirós, The Maias
William Empson, 7 Types of Ambiguity
Mathias Énard, Compass
Tell Them of Battles, Kings & Elephants
Shusaku Endo, Deep River
Jenny Erpenbeck, The End of Days
Go, Went, Gone
Lawrence Ferlinghetti
A Coney Island of the Mind
F. Scott Fitzgerald, The Crack-Up
On Booze
Jean Frémon, Now, Now, Louison
Rivka Galchen, Little Labors
Forrest Gander, Be With
Romain Gary, The Kites
Natalia Ginzburg, The Dry Heart
Happiness, as Such
Henry Green, Concluding
Felisberto Hernández, Piano Stories
Hermann Hesse, Siddhartha
Takashi Hiraide, The Guest Cat
Yoel Hoffmann, Moods
Susan Howe, My Emily Dickinson
Debths
Bohumil Hrabal, I Served the King of England
Qurratulain Hyder, River of Fire
Sonallah Ibrahim, That Smell
Rachel Ingalls, Binstead's Safari
Mrs. Caliban
Christopher Isherwood, The Berlin Stories
Fleur Jaeggy, Sweet Days of Discipline
Alfred Jarry, Ubu Roi
B.S. Johnson, House Mother Normal
James Joyce, Stephen Hero
Franz Kafka, Amerika: The Man Who Disappeared
Investigations of a Dog
Yasunari Kawabata, Dandelions
John Keene, Counternarratives
Heinrich von Kleist, Michael Kohlhaas
Alexander Kluge, Temple of the Scapegoat
Taeko Kono, Toddler-Hunting
Laszlo Krasznahorkai, Satantango
Seiobo There Below
Ryszard Krynicki, Magnetic Point
Eka Kurniawan, Beauty Is a Wound
Mme. de Lafayette, The Princess of Clèves
Lautréamont, Maldoror
Siegfried Lenz, The German Lesson
Denise Levertov, Selected Poems